THE CURE

JASON MAILEY

authorHOUSE®

AuthorHouse™
1663 Liberty Drive
Bloomington, IN 47403
www.authorhouse.com
Phone: 833-262-8899

Published by AuthorHouse 06/13/2023

ISBN: 979-8-8230-1002-3 (sc)
ISBN: 979-8-8230-1001-6 (hc)
ISBN: 979-8-8230-1000-9 (e)

Library of Congress Control Number: 2023911019

Printed in the United States of America

Contents

Chapter 1

Acolyte Facility

Dr. Rachael Morgan, a beautiful, headstrong, black-haired woman, was eager for a chance to put her name on a major scientific breakthrough. Rachael was approached by Jessica Price, a scientist who also happened to be the vice president's wife. She approached Rachael about working on a project that had some meaning. Rachael knew Ms. Price was using her eagerness to recruit her to her own team. Rachael had heard she had taken credit for things she didn't do because of her husband. Rachael didn't care. But she would soon find out that working for Ms. Price could take you to places you just shouldn't go.

Brent, the head of security for the Acolyte Facility, opened the door, letting Jessica and her security guard into Rachael's office. As she walked in, Brent announced from the door, "Here is Jessica, ma'am." Brent closed the door behind her, muttering under his breath, "Bitch."

"Rachael, I want those results from the tests you ran. You did start the human trials just like we discussed, didn't you?" Jessica requested.

"Yes, we did start human trials, even though I strongly disagreed with it in my emails to you. The side effects are showing very extreme results this early in the testing phase," Dr. Morgan said, looking up from her desk to see Price and another person standing next her. Dr. Morgan stopped talking midsentence after seeing the other person.

"Don't worry about her. She is the head of security at my facility and can be trusted. Let me introduce you to Marissa," Jessica said.

Marissa stepped forward and shook Dr. Morgan's hand. She was a lovely young woman with straight blond hair and green eyes; many had mistaken her as no threat because of her looks. Nevertheless, she used to be in the army as a military police officer, and she could knock a six-foot man on his back in seconds with ease.

"I have General Rhodes coming to inspect these test subjects and see the results," Price informed Dr. Morgan.

"The military! What do they want with this cure?" Rachael yelled angrily.

Just then, General Rhodes came in through the door, just in time to catch the last part of the conversation. "Dr. Morgan, we want this to help people, too. If we can get this distributed, we can save lives, and this will not be just for our troops if that's what you're thinking," Rhodes said, directing his words toward Rachael.

"This is my project. I should have the right to know what the military wants with this cure," Rachael said, the anger still in her voice.

"Rachael, who do you think all the funding comes from?" Jessica said, matching Rachael's anger.

"Just for the record, our animal testing wasn't successful. Testing the human and animal genes is where we are having difficulties. I think we need to do more testing, but Jessica has told me to push forward." Rachael looked directly at the general, who didn't seem to care about what she was saying.

Rachael sighed and kept walking toward the subjects. Arriving at the end of hall, they entered Lab 1A, where the subjects were held. They walked in to see a green fluid glowing in a vial. A label at the bottom of the vial read, "Compound Z." Dr. Morgan picked up the chart on the table and handed it to General Rhodes. On the top, it was marked, "Subject 1."

"After infecting subject 1 with H1N1, we gave the subject Compound Z. The results were amazing. After ten minutes, the flu was gone," Rachael explained.

"Was the subject cured?" Jessica asked curiously.

"Yes, but the side effects made the subject even worse afterward—vomiting; fever; and, ultimately, death. Same for the second subject," Rachael said.

"But the H1N1 was cured?" Jessica said.

"Yes, but didn't you hear me? They died." Rachael handed over the subjects' charts.

"It happens in all studies," Jessica said unsympathetically, looking at the charts. "What about some of the staff who we used the lower doses on? I think it was Compound X as you named it. What where the results there?" she asked eagerly.

"Out of the four who got the dose, Brent was the only survivor. His brother died, and a pilot died as well. Nancy, a friend, died from this as well. She volunteered for the shot. She was convinced this was the cure. I regret this, and I've informed her husband that she is sick, not dead. Brent's DNA somehow accepted the compound into his system; his blood now has a black tint. In one of the studies, my employees were attacked. Brent went into the room, and it was like the infected subjects didn't even know he was there. That's how he was able to deal with them. He needs to be studied more." Rachael showed her findings on her tablet.

"OK," Jessica said, glancing over at the general. "Keep going with the other subjects."

"For subjects 3 and 4, we lowered the dosage of Compound Z, and right now they have small fevers—nothing too serious. We are watching for any signs like before." Rachael again showed the information on her tablet.

"So, it works?" Jessica asked.

"We still need weeks of testing because of subject 5," Rachael said.

"And what's wrong with subject 5?" General Rhodes questioned.

"Subject 5 is the first to receive the low-dosage injections. Well, see for yourself." Rachael sound frightened.

When Rachael pulled back the curtain, subject 5 ran toward the glass and was stopped by restraints that cut into his skin like a razor blade. This didn't seem to bother the subject. His skin looked pale, like a piece of chicken that had been left out in the sun to rot. His eyes seemed to be bleeding, though it wasn't blood but, rather, a black ooze running down his face. His eyes looked gray. His pupils were gone. The two women stepped back, but the general just stayed in place, not fazed by what he saw, looking down at the chart hanging on the window.

"It says on these charts the subject died," the general said after shuffling through the charts.

"That's correct, sir. The subject did die, and half an hour later, the subject came back and attacked my staff. Two of my staff were bitten, and one nearly lost an eye. The subject then broke the restraints and clawed at their faces. All my staff are being treated for their injuries; we need more testing." Rachael's face saddened as she remembered her staff.

"You're saying he came back to life. If this is possible, just think of the possibilities. If we can bring someone back, this could be groundbreaking." Jessica looked at the subject tied up and started to think about the possibilities.

"Yes, I can see it now. Come back to life but become a psychopath. I don't think that's something we can say is a side effect. Look at his face. He's dead. Even you can see that," Rachael said, thinking that this was a mistake.

"There are side effects with all medication. That's why we list them on the bottle. The other two you said show no signs like this, just a fever." Jessica looked down at the charts of the other patients.

"Yes, Jessica, we do put side effects on labels, not that you will possibly die and come back and become crazy." To Rachael, it seemed Jessica didn't care about people, just results, and it made her uneasy.

"When you said the subject broke other restraints, you mean the subject's strength has increased?" General Rhodes said, lost in his thoughts about what this could do for his soldiers.

His thoughts were cut short by the sound of Rachael's voice. "Yes, but also subject aggression. The restraints were weakened by his thrashing around, and they snapped. Myself, and my assistants, Ed and Monica, agree we need to bring this back down to formula and start over." Rachael looked over at Jessica.

"*Start over*! It works. We need to move forward with more subject testing," Jessica said, looking over at the general.

"I will not sign off on that. Are you crazy, Jessica?" Rachael looked concerned.

"Rachael, please leave the room so that Price and I can have a word," the general said, looking at Marissa.

As Marissa escorted Rachael out of the room, Rachael looked back over her shoulder at them. "Good," she yelled. "Maybe you can talk some sense into her."

Just before exiting the room, when Jessica and Rhodes both had their attention on the charts, Rachael surreptitiously pressed active coms in the room. Now she listened.

"Jessica, we have an opportunity here. Just think. With a little tweaking of this so-called cure, we could make soldiers that are stronger and more aggressive. We just point them at the target and let them go. This could really help you with your funding if done right," General Rhodes said, turning but still looking at subject 5.

"Perhaps you're right. Do you know where we can get more subjects for testing?" Jessica asked.

"I know a little town just outside of Austin," General Rhodes said, looking at the vial of green liquid on the table. Picking it up, he examined it closely.

"I want to give you both Compound Z and Compound X to use. The results would be interesting." As she said this, Jessica went over to the fridge and grabbed another vial. This one, its contents a bright blue, was labeled "Compound X." She closed the fridge, revealing a sign on the front of the glass, marking it classified. She walked over and handed General Rhodes the vial and then turned to look at subject 5. She was filled with excitement and curiosity.

Rachael opened the door hard and blew past Marissa.

"Are you both crazy!? Did you see what was happening to these subjects? They are all dying or dead, and all you can think about is how to use it," Rachael said, yelling.

"This project is now under military control and is classified, so any word of this, and it's your ass, Rachael," Jessica said, glancing over to the general.

"Listen, Rachael, it's not just about this. It's also to see how we can deal with this virus if it gets released and see what happens in a real-life situation. It's also about seeing how it will affect other people—if it makes them stronger, faster. Just think of the possibilities." General Rhodes was trying to keep his excitement from his voice and failing.

"OK. What if you can't contain it?" Rachael asked, looking at them both.

"You let me worry about that. Nice working with you, Doc," the general said. With that, he left the room, giving Rachael a small smile on the way out.

"Fuck you, asshole," Rachael shouted in reply. She turned to Jessica. "You can't do this, Jessica. What are we supposed to do now? We get thrown out like trash?"

"Keep working with these subjects. And keep me informed of their status. If and when they pass, I will find you more subjects," Jessica said, starting to get annoyed with Rachael.

"What about Brent? His injections have made him more aggressive. I think he suspects we had a hand in his brother's death," Rachael said, waiting for a reply as Jessica paced back and forth, thinking.

"His part in this is over. Dispose of him," Jessica replied, looking at Rachael. "We can't have any loose ends."

"How am I supposed to do that?" Rachael replied, thinking she was no killer and also thinking that too many people had died already.

"I don't care. It's up to you," Jessica replied, walking out.

As Jessica stepped out into the hall through the door, she saw that Marissa was on a satellite phone and that she shut it off immediately upon seeing her.

"Who was that?" Jessica asked, interested.

Marissa's hands shook with nervousness as she replied. "Oh nothing. Just checking in with our facility." Marissa's voice shook a little, and then she got her confidence back. "Are we ready to go, ma'am?"

Jessica and Marissa got into her personal chopper and left the facility.

As she entered the chopper, she looked at her phone. Seeing that General Rhodes had called her, she called him back.

"Do you think Rachael will be an issue?" the general asked, his voice sounding concerned.

"No. She will play ball. She can't afford to lose this job. If not, I will handle it." Jessica hoped she was right.

"Be sure you, do," the general said, hanging up the phone abruptly.

Rachael walked into her office. Monica, her lead assistant, was waiting. She saw Rachael's face in a kind of snarl that she had never seen before. She thought Jessica must have pissed her off.

"Rachael, I need to speak with you." Monica's voice sounded panicked.

"What is it, Monica? I don't have time," she replied, annoyed.

"It's subjects 3 and 4."

"And what about them? Did their fever break?"

"No, ma'am. They both died."

"What? They both had a mild fever. What the hell happened?"

"Organs just shut down, and they collapsed, both dead."

"I want a full blood work up ASAP. Got it?" Rachael said angrily.

The intercom sparked to life. Ed's voice was frantic on the other end. "Turn your security camera to the morgue now."

"What is it, Ed?" Rachael replied as she flipped her camera to the morgue and saw subjects 1 and 2 ripping their way out of their bags.

Monica yelled to Ed, "Get to Rachael's office now."

Rachael picked up her walkie, frantic. "Security, get to the morgue *now*! We have a situation."

"Yeah what is it? Another doctor get locked out again?" Brent was laughing at other end of the walkie.

"No. Subjects 1 and 2 just ripped out of their bags and are attacking the staff," Rachael yelled over the walkie, frantic.

"You heard her. *Move*!" Brent yelled to his security guards, adding into the walkie, "On our way. Lock yourself down in your office. We will let you know when it's all clear."

"How many security staff do we have?" Monica asked, staring at the monitors.

"We have eight. Hopefully, it's enough to restrain two of them. That's not what scares me," Rachael explained, still looking at the monitors focused on the morgue.

"What scares you?" Monica asked, still watching the monitors.

"What scares me is what happens if they fail? Because we have two more subjects who could wake up at any moment."

Ed ran into the office. "Are you guys seeing this?" he asked, now looking at the monitors with them.

Rachael, Monica, and Ed watched the security cameras. Monica shrieked as she watched another staff member trying to fight off one of the infected. One of the infected jumped on a morgue staff member, and blood sprayed everywhere.

"Holy shit. They're dead. *Where the hell is security*?!" Monica screamed, a look of horror crossing her face and tears starting to fall down her cheeks.

"Calm down, Monica. They will get there," Rachael said, though she was thinking the same thing. And now she was yelling at Ed. "Ed, lock down the morgue."

"But there are two workers still in there." Ed hesitated before pushing the button.

Looking at the screen, Rachael knew that, if she had Ed lock down that morgue, her friends who she had worked with for the past few months would die. Her head was swimming and her heart pounded in her chest like a jackhammer. She thought if this kept up, her heart would beat out of her chest. She glanced over to Ed, not realizing that tears had begun to stream down her face. "Lock it down," she said, her voice cracking from emotion.

Ed saw her internal struggle and her tears. He knew her decision came with a very heavy heart and hit the button on the screen to lock the area down.

Sally in the morgue pleaded for them to open the area, yelling into the speaker and pounding her fists on the door while the infected were attacking some of her friends. "Please open the door. I don't want to die. Please." Her thoughts were no longer of her friends but, instead, of her daughter. Tears fell down her face. She now feared she would never see her again, and she pounded on the door again.

"Sorry. You know we can't do that. We can't do that," Rachael replied, trying to keep her composure as she slowly turned off the coms.

Monica reached for a button, but Rachael slapped Monica's hand away.

"She's going to die," Monica yelled, tears streaming down her face. She knew Sally. The two of them had had lunch together and had shared stories.

"Monica, if one of those things get out, we could be next," Ed said, trying to comfort her.

As they were looking at the monitor, one of the infected subjects grabbed Sally, biting her neck, making blood squirt everywhere. Throwing her to the ground, the creature bared its teeth and then bit into her arm, coming up with a chunk of flesh in its mouth. Monica looked away, crying.

"You're a murderer, Rachael," Monica began. But one look at her face told her Rachael's decision was already haunting her, and she stepped back.

"Look at the screen," Rachael said, pointing.

"Holy shit. No. That's not possible." Ed's jaw dropped.

"What is it?" Monica said, turning back to the monitors.

They watched as the three morgue workers who had just been killed got back up to their feet. "It's impossible," Ed said, looking at the screen.

Rachael grabbed the walkie. "*Security, do not enter the room. I repeat, do not enter the room!*" Rachael yelled into the walkie, adding, "Damn these stupid walkies," when only static came back.

"There are now five infected, not two. Do you read me?" Rachael said, frantically trying the walkie once more.

"They're all going to die, aren't they?" Monica said, sobbing.

Brent Adams hated his job as security leader. Week after week, he would sit in his security office and wait for a call. Most of the time, it was a call about a worker leaving the security clearance key in a room, and he or one of his security officers had to open it. It was Brent and seven others for this facility. He'd served two tours in the army, and this place was started to get boring compared to what he used to do. He had once been part of an elite team that had helped track down and eliminate al Qaeda operators.

After he'd gotten out, his brother, Kent, had asked him if he wanted to make some real money as a soldier for hire. All he had to do was help protect some stupid facility. After getting there, both were told they had to be inoculated. After a while, his brother had gotten sick and died, and now he found himself always upset and angry. He blamed Rachael. She was the one who had given them the shot; she was going to pay. He was beginning to think he would never see any action, but lately his job had become interesting.

After the call came through about subjects attacking staff members, he ordered his team to grab the restraints and the shock sticks and their guns. But Brent grabbed the AR15 with a grenade launcher. He'd specifically asked for this weapon because it was what he'd used in the army.

"Let's move out. Go," Brent said to his security team.

"Sir, you really think we're going to need guns?"

"I don't know. Just keep moving. We will see when we get there."

"Sir, why are they in the morgue? I mean, I thought they were dead, sir."

"Shut the fuck up and get ready to breach," Brent yelled.

"Rachael, we're at the morgue door," he said into the walkie. "Do you read me?"

When he got no reply, he cursed. "Fucking radio is out." Then he quickly made a decision. "Fuck it. Team, we go in by twos. Restraints ready. I will have cover fire. On my mark, breach."

Seven men waited behind Brent for the signal.

"Go." Brent opened the door. As he was the first one in, he stopped and saw pools of blood, as if someone had turned the sprinklers on in the room, only they were full of blood. Among the pools of blood were chunks of flesh that looked partially eaten. The sight started to break something free in him. His thought popped like a bubble as one of the men came in behind him yelling.

"What the fuck happened in here?" the guard said upon seeing all the blood.

Brent pointed at on one of the infected coming at them.

The team quickly slipped into the room, prepared to take down the first subject.

"Two of you check the next room now," Brent ordered, and two of the guards ran into the next room.

Brent walked over to the infected his men had just restrained and rolled it over with his foot. Its eyes looked gray, and blood dripped down its face from its eyes and ears. Its mouth was still trying to snap at him.

Looking down, the guard jumped back. "Holy fuck. That's subject 1. We put him here just a few hours ago. He was dead."

Screams came from the other room where the two security personnel had gone to scout. Brent ran into the room where he'd just sent two of his security officers and screamed as he looked at the horror around him. His men had been ripped apart by these things. Suddenly, he remembered the gun in his hands, and he opened fire. He pumped round after round into the chests of the creatures eating his men.

He held down the trigger until the gun ran dry.

Just as Brent turned around, he saw two more of his men taken down from behind.

The other three ran for the door, but it was locked. Brent fell to his knees, knowing they were all dead.

"Ed, what is going on in that other room? Switch cameras now."

"Holy shit. They're getting torn apart in there," Ed said as he watched in horror.

"Lock that room down again, now damn it," Rachael yelled, her head swimming.

"You will be killing them," Ed replied, hesitating.

"They're already dead, Ed. They just don't know it. So just do it," Rachael yelled again.

Ed hit the lockdown button once again.

One of the guards got to the door and began pounding on it after it didn't open with his key, yelling, "Please let us out. We're going to fucking die in here."

Another security officer had been yelling into the radio, and now his voice became a panicked squeal.

"I can't. They might get out," Rachael yelled back on the radio.

More screams could be heard in the background.

"You fucking bitch. Let us out." Now, tears were streaming down the security officer's face.

"Look. Subjects 3 and 4 are now moving in their bags. Just let them out please," Monica yelled, tears rolling down her face still. "Please, Rachael. They're all going to die. *Please, Ed*! Do something."

"I can't. Rachael's right. If just one of those things gets loose, we could all be dead." Ed's voice was low, and his head hung down.

"*You are fucking cowards*!" Monica ran into next office, crying.

As the security officers stood next to the door pleading, they didn't see the infected behind them. One of them started to scream as they were dragged to the floor.

Brent knew protocol, and he knew they were dead.

He stood up with his gun. "Fuck it," he said and loaded a grenade round into his AR15.

"*Get the fuck down,*" Brent yelled to the last remaining security officers.

Ed was watching the screen to the morgue as Brent loaded the grenade round into his gun. "Rachael, we have a problem happening in the morgue."

"What is it now, Ed?" Rachael said, sounding just done with everything.

Ed answered frantically. "It's Brent. He just loaded a fucking grenade round into his gun. I think he's going to blow up the door."

Rachael quickly grabbed the radio. "Brent," Rachael yelled into the walkie, "you can't do this. Protocol states that the infection can't leave the room. You hear me, Brent?"

Brent picked up his walkie.

Before he could answer, something broke loose in his head—like a dam that was no longer holding back a sea, anger rolled over him. And he felt free. He let all of it go—his feeling toward her, Dr. Morgan, the one he blamed for his brother's death. He didn't care anymore, not even for his own men, who were being attacked and killed around him. He held the walkie up to his mouth and replied, "Fuck protocol, bitch." Brent aimed and fired the weapon at the door, saying under his breath, "Fuck you all."

The grenade shell hit the door, exploding on contact and sending flames and alarms blazing. The blast was so powerful in the small space it knocked back the two security personnel closest to the door and all infected nearby. One of the men took some debris from the door and glass in his throat and started choking on his own blood. Brent started to walk out the door.

The other man yelled, "Aren't you going to help us, Brent?"

Brent turned around and smiled. "It's everyone for themselves." And he kept walking down the hall toward the security office.

Just as Brent left the morgue, the man he had been talking to was overwhelmed with infected. He screamed while he was ripped apart.

Monica walked out of the back room. Tears still in her eyes, she sniffled as she asked, "Hey, what are you guys looking at? What's wrong?" she pressed when their faces remained blank.

"I'll tell what's wrong. Brent just let all the infected out, and now we're fucked."

"We must close the panic doors on both sides of us down the hall," Ed said to Rachael.

"Well, while you both have been in here, I think I've come up with something," Monica said, sniffling. "Going over the Compound Z files, I remembered that Compound V would make Compound Z null and erase it. If we can just manipulate Compound V, we could make it a vaccine to fight Compound Z."

"That would be great, Monica, if we still had it," Rachael said with anger in her voice. "Right now, we need to focus on the task at hand, so those things don't get in here. Got it?"

"Yes, ma'am," Monica replied, her head down.

"So, Ed. What do we need to do to close these panic doors?" Rachael asked, looking concerned.

"One of us has to go to the south corridor and one to the north corridor and close them with our access codes. I'll take north. Rachael, you take south. After I close mine, I'm going to look for Brent. He might be able to help us. Or at least he might have some weapons I can use," Ed said.

"Are you crazy? Brent just blew the door open, and you want to find him to, what, have a talk? He will kill you," Monica said, staring at her colleague with a puzzled expression.

"If I can get the drop on him, maybe I can take him out. I think he will come for us because we locked that door." Ed sounded a little uneasy about his own plan.

"Just for the record, I think this is a bad idea. Stay safe OK," Monica said, trying to smile.

"Sounds like a plan. Hold on." Rachael walked over to her desk and entered a code. "Here take one of these." She tossed Ed a pistol.

"Thanks," Ed replied.

Just before Ed walked out the door, Monica ran over to him. "Be careful," she whispered. "I'm sorry I called you a coward." She kissed him on his cheek.

"No problem," Ed replied. "I know you didn't mean it."

Ed walked out the door wearing a grin from ear to ear.

As Ed made his way down the south corridor, he saw Brent coming and ducked down around the corner, holding his breath and hoping Brent, the man who had just let the infected out of the morgue, didn't see him.

As Brent strolled by, Ed swore he heard him mumbling under his breath, "I'm going to kill them all."

After Brent was out of sight, Ed blew out a large breath. *Holy shit*, he thought to himself. *Now that was close.*

Ed reached the panic door and entered his activation code. For a moment, nothing happened, and he started to get nervous. He could now hear muffled noises—moaning and then what sounded like screams.

"Come on, you stupid door," Ed said to himself.

Just then, the door started to close, and his panic subsided.

He turned around, heart still pounding, to follow Brent to the security office.

Rachael was ready to go down her corridor and was just about to step out of her office when Monica spoke.

"Rachael, what should I do while you're gone?"

Rachael looked annoyed. "Just keep this place locked down until Ed or I get back. Think you can handle that?"

"Yes, ma'am," Monica replied.

As Rachael walked down her hall, she walked by some of the viewing rooms where Nancy and the other pilot had been kept. Both had turned into those things, thrashing about. Rachael couldn't help but feel for Nancy. After all, she was a friend, as was her husband.

Nancy's husband, that's it. How could I forget? she thought to herself. *First things first, the panic door.*

Rachael arrived at the panic door and entered her code. "Denied," the panel by the door read right away, and she tried again.

She tried it again and again. She couldn't remember her code, and now she was hearing screams down the corridor.

It hit her like a ton of bricks. Ed had used his ID for the lockdown. She entered his code. "Granted," the screen read. Though she felt some relief, the door wasn't closing.

She glanced down the hall and saw a figure coming at her. It was gaining speed, and then she heard the moan. She raised her gun, aimed, and pulled the trigger. It was a perfect shot, right into the chest. But the creature didn't fall. In fact, it didn't even same fazed.

She lined up her shot again, this time putting two rounds through the advancing creature's heart. *It should be dead*, she thought to herself upon firing the third round straight through its chest.

The creature picked up speed as it made its way toward her.

Finally, the doors started closing. Rachael lined up her last shot, this time aiming at its head, and fired. The creature went down just as the doors closed.

"That's it," she said to herself. "You have to shoot them in the head."

She started walking back to her office. She had a plan that might just work.

Ed followed Brent down the hall and saw him go into the security office. Ed crept in right behind him.

"Put your hands up, Brent," Ed said with his heart beating and hands shaking, holding the gun in both hands.

"Or what?" Brent replied, still not facing him.

"I'll shoot you, you sick fuck."

Brent laughed. "And just why am I the sick fuck?"

"Because you let out the infection," Ed replied. "Now put your hands up."

"I'll tell you what's sick, Ed—locking us in that room with the infected. I had no choice," Brent said, turning to look at Ed.

"You always have a choice, Brent," Ed said. "And your choice might have killed us all. You know the protocol. You needed to stay in there until help arrived."

Brent laughed again. "What you really mean is I was supposed do just die in there and wait for someone to pick up my corpse. Well fuck that, Ed. I'm not going out like that. I'm not the bad guy here, Ed. Rachael and that bitch Price are. They created these infected things that killed all your friends in the morgue. We're the same, you and me, Ed." Brent grinned.

"We're nothing alike," Ed replied.

"Sure we are, Ed. You took this job to be close to your crush, Rachael. Didn't you? Even though that's not company policy. Isn't that right, Ed? See, Ed, we're both rule breakers. You want to fuck your boss, and I let out the infected."

"That's not the same thing," Ed replied, hands still shaking.

"Sure it is, Ed. You say potato. I say potahto. With the world going to hell in a handbasket, I could even help you fuck her. And I'll fuck the little slut Monica." Brent's tone had a little giggle in it, and he smiled again as he looked at Ed.

Ed replied angrily, "Don't talk about them like that, you sick fuck."

"Ahh, you like them both, don't you, Ed?" Brent said with a laugh.

"Just because we have a problem in here doesn't mean it will get out," Ed said, sweating now, his gun really shaking.

"She didn't tell you, did she?" Brent laughed again.

Ed yelled, "Get on your knees."

"I didn't know you liked men too. Now who's the sick fuck?" Brent replied, laughing again.

"Your project has been scrapped. The military took it over to do some testing of their own in the field. She didn't tell you?"

"You're lying," Ed replied.

"I'm in the security office, Ed. I hear and see everything I want to." Brent pointed to the security system behind Ed.

Ed moved closer to Brent and started to reach for the restraints on Brent's belt. When, just for a second, he took his eye off Brent to grab the restraints, Brent grabbed the arm Ed had the gun in with his right hand. With his left arm, he delivered a blow to Ed's head, knocking him backward and causing him to drop the gun.

"Well, Ed, we could have had some fun," Brent said with an evil laugh. "I guess I'll have some by myself." With a huge right hand to Ed's face, Brent knocked him out.

Rachael ran back into her office, startling Monica.

"Is everything all right?" Monica asked.

Rachael replied, "Nancy."

"What about her?" Monica asked.

"She has a husband, Dr. Bradley, right?" Rachael asked.

"Yes," Monica replied.

"Remember she sent those Compound V containers to her husband because she wanted him to bring them here so she could see her, that scientist."

"Yes, now I remember. If he still has them, he can bring them here, and we can see if my idea works," Monica replied. "But he is so busy. How will you get him to come here? Are you going to tell him what's going on here?"

"No. I'll tell him Nancy's super sick, and she wants to see him. Give me that satellite phone. I have a call to make."

Rachael hung up the phone.

"Are you crazy, Rachael? What happens when he gets here and Nancy's dead?" Monica asked.

"We tell him things took a turn for the worst. We just really need that Compound V if we're going to fix this."

"I guess you're right," Monica replied. "I wonder where Ed is at."

"I'm sure he's fine," Rachael said.

"I sure hope so."

Just then, the intercom in Dr. Morgan's office came on.

"Hello, ladies. Ed and I are having a wonderful time," Brent said.

"Holy shit. That's Brent," Rachael said.

"Don't worry. Once I'm done with Ed, I will be joining you."

"Can't wait."

Laughter sounded over the intercom.

Chapter 2

The Mission

Captain Steven Miller was starting to feel old—and not only feeling it but also seeing it. His face was getting wrinkled, and more and more gray could be found in his hair. Now, he'd been asked to do one more mission by his old commander, General Rhodes—who he'd heard was now working in the classified sector. He could have told the general no, but he wanted to prove to himself he still had it. And he needed to convince an old friend, Sergeant Smith, to help one more time. He guessed his weekend in Vegas would just have to wait.

"I had a week of vacation planned in Vegas for some R and R and have been called back on this assignment. What about you, Sergeant? Did you have any plans?" Captain Miller asked.

"Well, Captain, I was going to see my son this weekend," Sergeant Smith replied.

The captain raised his brows. "I'm sorry I pulled you away from that."

"His mom is a crackhead. He stays with his grandma and grandpa. He will be fine, just as long as he's not with her. Besides, what are old pals for?" the sergeant replied.

"I hear you." Captain Miller shook his head. "Let's go; briefing in five."

General Rhodes strode into the briefing room. He looked even older than the captain remembered, but he still had muscle—he had aged like a side of beef left out in the sun.

"Officer on deck!" Smith shouted, and they all rose as a unit.

Rhodes walked past the rigid soldiers. As he passed Miller, the younger man thought he saw a bit of stiffness in that regal step. Was the old man finally breaking down? Well, if he was, it couldn't come too soon, Miller thought.

"At ease, men," Rhodes said. "Sorry to cut your plans short, but we have a special assignment that couldn't wait."

Miller sat rigidly. He'd been on one too many trips to believe the old goat when he said he was sorry. He was never sorry, and Miller knew better than to plan anything that couldn't be canceled. His failed marriage had taught him that much.

Rhodes didn't elaborate. He seemed to be waiting for something.

Just as the tension pushed to that uncomfortable point, the rear door opened, and two soldiers walked in.

Rhodes motioned to a pair of seats up front. "Corporal Hicks, Private Dickson, glad you could make it." In the nearly empty room, it seemed almost comical that the general had to suggest they ignore the other thirty odd seats and just sit up front.

Once the newcomers were seated, Rhodes continued. "What I'm about to tell you is eyes only. The four of you are not to speak about it to anyone else without a clear, expressed, and lawful order."

Four of them? Miller didn't like the sound of that. He liked the look of Hicks and Dickson even less. Dickson was a nervous guy, well, more of a kid. His curly red hair and freckles probably made him look younger than he was, but even with that, Miller doubted he was over twenty. The kid chewed his nails and squirmed in his seat. First time out? Probably. *Great.* Miller didn't look forward to babysitting.

He turned his attention to Hicks. If anything, the corporal seemed even worse. Even at ease, he remained ramrod straight, his shaved head a by-the-books cut from a past era. His tight jaw clinched, giving an already angular face an unflattering, chiseled look.

The general turned to address all of them. "Now, about the mission. The four of you need to recon this small town just outside Austin. All citizens are reported missing," Rhodes said, pointing at the map.

Captain Miller and Sergeant Smith glanced at each other and then looked back at the general.

"Sir, that sounds like a job for local law enforcement, sir. Why did we get called in?" Captain Miller asked, looking puzzled.

The general hesitated before continuing, like he was thinking of a bullshit answer. Captain Miller had seen that look many times. "We would leave it to them, but all law enforcement who were sent in have not come back, and the army is too busy right now. So, I recommended you. You're the best recon guys we have." The general cleared his throat importantly and went on. "The whole town is quarantined. You need to go to the quarantine zone and meet up with a citizen who knows the town—Rodriguez. He will help you navigate it. However, your top priority is to find out what happened there and get your asses back to the extraction zone, you understand?"

"Sir, yes, sir."

"Dismissed!"

"General, one last thing." Miller cleared his throat. "Why is this town quarantined, sir?" he asked.

Again, the general looked at him, thinking about an answer to give. "Captain, that is classified," the general snapped. "Just get in there and find out what happened."

"Yes, sir," Captain Miller replied, glancing at the sergeant again.

As the general walked out of earshot, Sergeant Smith leaned in and murmured, "Captain, this is bullshit, man. He is telling us there is no army to do this, and he recommended us? Something sounds fishy to me, Captain. Have you heard of anything like this before?"

Captain Miller slowly shook his head. "Sergeant, I have been on lots of classified missions, but this just smells bad."

Sergeant Smith muttered under his breath as he and the captain strode to the bulwark to collect their gear. "Where are these guys, Captain? Oh, here they come in the chopper," he added, more to himself than anyone else.

As the two men approached the landing aircraft, they saw one of their new companions hop to the deck. There were no insignias on his uniform. As he approached, his red hair was short and curly like a true ginger.

The private straightened and approached them before raising an inexperienced salute. "Private Dickson reporting for duty, sir."

Captain Miller eyed the man up and down, feeling old. This kid looked even younger in the daylight. "How old are you, son?"

"I'm twenty-one, sir," he replied, still stiff as a board.

"At ease. This is Sergeant Smith." The captain threw a thumb over his shoulder, aiming at where Smith was standing. Dickson looks over the captain's shoulder, and Smith gave him a nod.

"Where are you from?"

"Carolina, sir." Dickson seemed a little more at ease.

"Get your gear, Private."

"Yes, sir," Dickson replied.

As the private turned back toward the chopper, Captain Miller added, "Where is Corporal Hicks?"

"He is coming, sir. Getting his gear."

"Get on the chopper behind me, Private. You too, Sergeant."

"Yes, sir," both replied.

The second army man approached with his duffel slung over his shoulder. He looked like pure muscle; had brown hair and blue eyes, the kind ladies liked; and wore a stupid grin on his face. "Corporal Hicks reporting for duty, sir."

Captain Miller didn't look amused as he approached the chopper. "At ease. Where are you from, Corporal?" Captain Miller asked.

"Alabama, sir," he replied, not really standing to attention but looking as if he didn't want to be here.

"Look sharp! Drop point coming up," Captain Miller announced.

They heard the pilot's instruction over the headset. "Thirty seconds! This is as far as I take you. Cannot get a good drop elsewhere—too many trees. Good luck, gentlemen. God be with you."

"All right, men, you heard. *Move.* Go, Corporal, you're on point. Quarantine zone is two clicks up this trail. Move out," the captain ordered.

"Why the quarantine, Captain? What happened in this place?" Private Dickson asked.

Captain shook his head, looking at the men. "Private, Rhodes told you everything he knows. Just keep moving." The captain turned to address the sergeant. "Sergeant, come over here. What is the name of the guy we're supposed to meet?"

"Rodriguez, sir."

"Who is he?" Hicks asked.

"A biohazard specialist who was supposed to be meeting us who knows this area well and will help us recon the town and get us the proper gear from the outpost," the captain replied. "Quarantine outpost just over there. *Move out*!"

As Hicks and Dickson patrolled forward, Smith asked, "Where the hell is everyone, Captain? I thought there was supposed to be a big outpost here. Where did everyone go?"

Hicks looked at his phone and his radio. "I have no signal of any kind here. What the fuck is going on?" He looked a little concerned.

"If this was a town under quarantine by the army, they would have blocked all communications here, but I'm not sure why I'm not getting anything from the military radios," Captain Miller said, also looking at his equipment.

"I don't know, Sergeant. Spread out and the check camp for anyone—and for Rodriguez, especially. Keep alert."

"Better come here, sir!" Private Dickson's voice carried across the field.

The captain and the sergeant exchanged a glance, and then they marched toward Dickson's call. "What is it, Private?" the captain asked when Dickson was in view.

"There is blood everywhere." Dickson looked pale, looking at not only blood but also limbs on the ground with no body to claim them, and the parts that were left behind had bite marks on them and some had the flesh hanging off them like they been gnawed on by an animal. Dickson added, "No bodies though."

"You don't look good," the sergeant said, putting his hand on Dickson's shoulder.

"Yeah, I'm good. Never seen so much blood before. That's all," Dickson replied, pulling himself together.

"Same here, sir," Hicks called from a few feet away. "Blood everywhere, What the fuck's going on?" He looked around before adding, "We should spread out and look for a command bunker to see if anyone is held up there."

"Good idea, Corporal. You're with me, Private. Sarge and Hicks, check the bunker on the left while we go right. Keep me posted," Captain Miller commanded.

"Yes sir!" both replied.

"Sergeant, we have a closed door; come back up," Captain Miller said, yelling down the tunnel. He pounded on the door. "Anyone in there? Hello?"

From the other side of the door came a voice. "Who is out there?"

"Captain Miller, Special Forces; let us in!"

There was a pause. "How do I know you're not one of them?"

Captain Miller glanced over at Sergeant Smith and waved for him to come closer.

"He said 'one of them.' You think there is another military presence here?" he whispered to the sergeant.

Behind the door, they could still here the man. "Are you still out there? I have guns and plenty of ammo behind here. If you don't go away, I will start shooting."

Hicks pounded on the door. "Let us in. Or we will break the door down."

The captain grabbed Hicks and pushed him backward. "I want you and Dickson to watch the opening. Make sure you don't see signs of any other military outfit. Got me?"

Then he turned his attention back to the door. "I'm Captain Miller with Special Forces out of Fort Myers on direct orders from General Rhodes. I am ordering you to open this door."

The door opened. Lieutenant Hayes of US Army Special Forces stepped out. He was a very fit man, with round glasses and black hair. "Sorry about that. I'm Lieutenant Hayes, Captain. Get in."

"What the hell is going on here, Lieutenant?" the captain asked as he and the other three men filed into the building. Looking around, they saw maps, bio gear, and a man lying unconscious on the floor.

"Well, sir, it started around 1800 hours. We were having a little party, and Captain Grimes told some of us he lost contact with the other outposts.

So, he sent Lieutenant Johnson, who is lying on the floor unconscious, along with two others to go and find out why we lost communication. We thought it was a malfunction. It's happened before, no biggie. So, about an hour went by. And suddenly, Johnson came running out of the woods yelling that they were all dead, and we couldn't understand him. The captain told me to take him to the bunker.

"About a half hour goes by, and we are not getting anywhere. Johnson still has not made any sense. Then we start hearing screaming, followed by gunfire. The captain tells me to stay with Johnson and Rodriguez. Not even thirty seconds goes by, and I hear shooting in the tunnel, and someone was pounding on the door yelling, 'Let us in.' And then I hear the captain yelling, 'Do not open that door.' Then it went silent. I was about to open the door when Johnson knocked me out. I just now finally woke up to the sound of you guys. However, if you want to find out what happened, you're going to have to wake up Johnson."

"Rodriguez, where is the bio gear you had for us?" Captain Miller asked.

Rodriguez looked puzzled. "The only gear I got was what I came with. Rhodes said you would have your own."

Captain Miller took Sergeant Smith to the corner of the bunker. "Something doesn't seem right. Either Rhodes isn't telling us everything, or he doesn't know what going on here. If we needed the bio stuff, he would have given it to us. He's not one to send his men unprepared."

Sergeant Smith looked back toward the other men. Whispering to Captain Miller, he said, "I agree. I think we should head back. I don't know if we are equipped to handle this. It's up to you."

Captain Miller looked down for a moment, pondering what Sergeant Smith had said and then looked him directly in his eyes, stating, "We need to push forward. What if someone is in that town and needs our help? Let's find out what Johnson knows and go from there."

Sergeant Smith nodded in agreement. They fist-bumped and went back toward the others.

Lieutenant Johnson's eyes started to open. Hicks gave him a slap on the face. Captain Miller gave Hicks a stern look as if to say, *Enough.* Hicks gave him a nod and stopped. "Come on, Lieutenant. Out with it," Hicks said, splashing some water from his canteen in the lieutenant's face.

Finally, Johnson looked at Hicks and then at Captain Miller. "Yes, sir," Johnson replied, still dazed.

"Tell me everything you remember," the captain directed.

"I think we need to just get out of here," Johnson replied. His voice sounded slurred and panicked.

Hicks slapped him again. "Come on. Out with it."

Captain Miller grabbed Hicks's hand and shoved him away. "Enough of that. Just tell us what you remember." The captain was looking straight at Johnson now.

"Well, two privates and I were sent to find out why we could not reach the other outpost on coms. No big deal. Radio goes out all the time. So, we were messing around when we heard screaming, followed by gunfire. We got up on this ledge for a better view. As I looked through my scope, I saw these things that looked like humans, but they couldn't be humans. They were killing everyone. I even saw one guy fire an entire clip into one of these things"—Johnson's voice escalated with panic—"and it just kept coming. Then one of the privates lost their footing and fell. They all heard him and started running at him. We opened fire, but they kept coming. When they got to the private, they started ripping him in half—they were eating him. So, the other private and I took off with them behind us. The private fell. I tried to cover, but they came too fast, just jumping on him. He never had a chance. I finally got back here to tell them, but no one would listen to me."

"Listen to you?! You were not making any sense, babbling about, 'They're dead!' We could not make out what you were saying," Hayes said.

"Enough," Sergeant Smith snapped. "Dickson, where did Rodriguez say the town is?"

"He says the town is about six miles down the path."

"You're not really thinking about going into town, are you?" Johnson asked, his voice on the verge of cracking and his body tensing up.

"Johnson, we still have a job to do. Hayes, Johnson, you're coming with us. Get your shit and be ready in fifteen minutes. Got it?"

"If we do not see what's going on, this thing could get worse, and many more people could die," Captain Miller added, taking over from there. "I do not want that on my head. Let's do this and get our asses back alive.

"OK, listen up. When we leave this bunker, everyone stays frosty. We cover each other's backs, and we'll make it back—all of us. Let's move out. Sergeant Smith, Hicks, you're on point. Go. Rodriguez, where is the town?"

"Just over that hill, Captain."

"Dickson, take out the drone. I want to see everything down there."

As Captain Miller spoke, Dickson unpacked the drone and started to fly over the town.

"Any movement?"

"No, sir. Nothing moving down there. Looks like a ghost town," Dickson said.

"OK. We're going to do a clean sweep through the main street. Hicks, Johnson, Sergeant, you take the left side. Dickson, Hayes, Rodriguez, and I will take the right. Stay on your toes. I do not want anybody to die on this mission. You get me?" Captain Miller ordered.

"Sir, yes, sir!" everyone replied.

"All right. Move like you got a purpose.

"Hayes, let's start sweeping. You go first through the door, followed by Dickson and then Rodriguez. And I'll take up the rear."

As they started to sweep through the buildings along the main street, they found nothing except what looked like smashed furniture and small amounts of blood splatter that indicated some sort of struggle. As they moved into the first house, Hayes stopped and held up his hand, indicating the others should halt.

"Hey, Captain, you might want to see this. Bring up Rodriguez," Hayes said, his voice sounding concerned.

As Captain Miller came up to the front behind Hayes, he saw a pool of blood mixed in with some type of black fluid.

"Looks like someone was killed here," Hayes said, looking up at Captain Miller.

The captain and Rodriguez bent down to examine the blood. "You ever seen anything like this?" Captain Miller said, glancing sharply at Rodriguez.

"No," he said, looking horrified. His jaw dropped open, and his eyes went wide at the sight of the black fluid. "Whoever was attacked shouldn't have survived with so much blood loss," Rodriguez said.

Captain Miller got up and started to look around the room.

"What are you looking for?" Dickson asked, looking over at the captain.

"Well, look, this guy was attacked and then is lying dead. The attacker gets up and runs off back out the door. Then as the blood pattern seems to show, the person lying here gets up and runs after the attacker. As Rodriguez pointed out, he should have still been lying here," Captain Miller said, pointing to the bloody footprints.

"Let's finish our sweep and meet up with the sergeant. Hayes, on you," the captain said, starting to move into the next building.

"Captain, we finished sweeping the houses. We found some signs of struggle but no bodies," Sergeant Smith said when the two groups met back on the main street.

"Everyone, move to the warehouse at end of the street," Captain Miller said. He pointed in the direction of the warehouse, and they moved toward it, guns drawn.

"Sergeant Smith, take Hicks and Hayes. Check out the other side of the warehouse."

"Yes, sir," the sergeant replied.

"Anything, Sergeant?"

"No, sir! Wait. Hold on. There is a lady here. Ma'am, are you injured? Hicks, move in. Hayes, watch our backs. Ma'am, are you injured? Ma'am what the fuck? Hicks, move back," the sergeant yelled.

As he yelled, Hicks saw the woman's face. It looked as if an animal had eaten half of her face, with skin hanging off in strips. Startled by the woman's face, he shot her in the head.

"Wait," the sergeant yelled.

Captain Miller and Dickson ran into the warehouse with their guns drawn, ready for anything. "What the hell was that shooting?" the captain said, looking at all three men.

"We found a woman, sir. Hicks shot her in the head," the sergeant replied.

"Why the hell did he do that?"

"Sir, she was all messed up. Her face was half gone, sir. She startled me," Hicks said.

"It looks like she was attacked by an animal, sir."

As they started to walk closer to the body, they saw that there were body parts everywhere.

"What the fuck was that?" Hicks yelled.

Hicks saw glass break in front of the warehouse. And then people, who looked very pale and were covered in blood, were charging at them. Everyone raised their guns as screams echoed in the warehouse.

"Shit, we got contact, sir. Open fire. Take them out now," Captain Miller yelled.

Everyone started to fire at the human figures running at them.

"Why aren't they staying down?" Hicks yelled as he started to reload his weapon.

Captain Miller changed strategy and shot one of the human-like creatures in the head, putting it down for good. "Aim for the head," he yelled out.

All the men did as ordered.

Soon, all the contacts were put down, and Captain Miller yelled to cease fire.

Just as all the firing stopped, Johnson ran in from the back door, looking scared and panicked. "Those things I saw at the camp are chasing me," he yelled.

Captain Miller looked over Johnson's shoulder. "Where the hell is Rodriguez?"

"I don't know. I thought he was behind me," Johnson replied, looking behind him.

Captain Miller pushed Johnson out of the way and yelled, "Sergeant Smith, with me. Everyone else, stay here."

Captain Miller and Sergeant Smith ran out to look for Rodriguez.

Hicks rolled a body over, and Dickson jumped backward. "Holy shit. What happened to his neck?"

The man's neck had a chunk missing, and you could see the back of his throat, with skin and bone showing around the wound.

Johnson walked over to another body, examining it. "Why does this one have black stuff around his mouth, and the others don't?"

"Looks like he has some kind of disease. He has black ooze coming from his mouth and eyes. Either that or he's a zombie." Hicks chuckled and looked at Dickson.

"Shut the fuck up, Hicks," Hayes said, annoyed.

"No. I think he may be right. That is why you can only shoot him or her in the head," Johnson said.

"Shit, that's what they are," Hicks said.

"How do you guys know that?" Dickson spoke in a low tone, like he was starting to get scared.

"Dickson, haven't you ever seen zombie movies, man? That's the only way you can kill them. That's why the people at the outpost had troubles killing them," Hicks explained.

Just as they were talking, the infected man with the black fluid on his mouth sat up, grabbed Johnson's hand, and bit it.

Johnson screamed, "Get it off of me."

But the teeth remained clamped down on his hand.

Hicks ran up and shot the once human creature two more times in the head—with no effect. He started hitting it with the butt of his gun until its brains were out on the ground and black fluid was leaking out of it as well.

Johnson grabbed his hand and quickly started wrapping it to stop the bleeding.

"Shit. Are you all right?" Dickson asked.

"What the hell you think? The fucking thing bit off my fucking pinky," Johnson yelled back, still wrapping his hand.

Captain Miller and Sergeant Smith ran around the corner and saw Rodriguez on the ground with one of the infected people ripping out his throat. Captain Miller raised his rifle and quickly shot the infected in the head before it could get up and turn on them. Captain Miller tried to hold pressure on the neck wound, but it was too late. Rodriguez died.

"Fucking coward Johnson," Sergeant Smith yelled.

Just as he said that, Captain Miller, who was still on one knee, saw Rodriguez's eyes open. Then Rodriguez sat up, blood running from his mouth and his wound. Captain Miller's instinct kicked in, and he immediately put a round in Rodriguez's head.

"What the fuck was that?" Sergeant Smith said, glancing with a look of concern at Captain Miller.

"I don't know. But I bet our friend the general knows more about what's going on here than he cared to tell us," the captain replied, looking down at Rodriguez's body.

As Captain Miller and Sergeant Smith returned, they saw Johnson. Captain Miller grabbed him and was about to start yelling when he looked down at his hand and then saw the infected with its brains all over the ground.

"What the hell happened here?" Captain Miller asked, letting go of Johnson.

"It just came back and bit his hand. Hicks shot it two more times in the head and finally had to beat it to death before it would let go," Hayes said.

"Captain Miller, come here. You might want to see this!" Sergeant Smith was looking down at one of the infected.

"What is it, Sergeant?" Captain Miller asked.

"It's some army guys, sir. What the fuck? I thought the general said the army was too busy. What are they doing here?" Sergeant Smith said.

"Johnson, come here," Captain Miller said, looking down at one of the bodies. "Is this one of the guys from one of the other outfits that you recognize?"

"He's not with us, but I do know they sent some guys in with some doctors or something. I'm not sure," Johnson said, still holding his hand.

"Pack up your gear. We're heading back to the outpost. We'll see if we can get command there. Be on your toes. I don't want anyone else getting killed. Let's move!"

"Where's Rodriguez?" Dickson asked, looking concerned.

"He didn't make it," Captain Miller said. "Let's go now," he yelled.

This is bullshit—no command, crazy-looking people. Why did I sign up for this shit? Dickson thought to himself.

Dickson had joined the military because that was what his friends were doing. He'd soon found his talent; it was marksmanship. He loved shooting but not the blood. As long as he was far away when he shoots his rifle, he felt OK about it. At least it was better than seeing the results. He quickly got a name for himself for shooting the bad guys. It was just like a game to him.

When he was recruited for special missions, he thought it was going to be like being a secret agent. But it wasn't. His first mission was with Captain Miller, and he'd already been way too close to the blood.

As they were walking, Hicks got in between Captain Miller and Sergeant Smith. He spoke quietly. "Hey, Johnson doesn't look so good. He's not going to turn into one of those things, right?"

Captain Miller and Sergeant Smith stopped and looked at each other's faces. Their eye locked in matching looks of concern. As their eyes went wide, both knew exactly what the other was thinking—Rodriguez.

"I don't know, Hicks," Captain Miller said.

Sergeant Smith was still looking at him. "Actually, you do know, sir. We saw it," Sergeant Smith said, looking at Captain Miller.

"What are you talking about, sir? Are you talking about Rodriguez?" Hicks asked, his voice cracking.

"We need to deal with this now, sir. Hicks is right. He's not looking so hot," Smith said, looking back at Johnson.

Captain Miller sighed. "Fine. Let me go talk to him." Captain Miller walked away, calling for Johnson to come over to talk to him.

"How is the hand, Johnson?" Captain Miller asked, looking at his hand and his face.

"Hurts like a bitch, sir," he said, looking pale and woozy.

As Johnson was talking, blood started coming out of his nose and eyes. Without even thinking about it, Captain Miller took his sidearm out. In a quick motion, like a gunslinger, he put one round between the lieutenant's eyes.

Everyone jumped back, startled by the gunshot and by seeing Johnson on the ground.

Dickson was the first to talk. "Why did you do that?" he asked, looking pale himself.

"He was infected and going to turn. That's what I would want anyone here to do for me. Now we need to move out and get to that extraction zone. We need to move *now*," Captain Miller barked even louder than normal, meaning he didn't want to discuss it further.

As the pilot of the chopper landed at the extraction point, he radioed to say there was no sign of anyone. He and his copilot were given instructions to wait twenty minutes. If no one arrived, then they were to return to base.

"I'm going to go take a leak, man," the copilot said, stepping out of the chopper.

"Don't go too far. We may need to dust off quick," the pilot said.

"Yeah, yeah. What are you, my mother?" the copilot replied, laughing and waved his hand.

Five minutes went by, and the pilot yelled out, "Come on, man. What the hell is taking so long? Are you taking a shit?"

He heard some rustling in the back and unhooked himself to look out the back door. Just as he did so, an infected jumped on him, biting into his neck. Blood sprayed, and the pilot was ripped out of the chopper.

"Hicks, get in there. Tell them we need to dust off now," Captain Miller yelled to Hicks.

Hicks ran to the chopper. As he got closer, he noticed blood on the ground around the bird. Raising his gun, he slowly approached the chopper and looked inside to see no pilots in the seats and lots of blood. Hicks signaled for Captain Miller to come up.

"What is it, Hicks?" Captain Miller started to say and then stopped, noticing the blood inside.

"What are we going to do now, sir?" Hicks asked, concerned.

"Sergeant Smith can pilot. Get in and get on one of the guns now," Captain Miller yelled.

"Incoming!" Sergeant Smith yelled.

"Everyone in," Captain Miller yelled, climbing in and taking a firing position. He started taking down the incoming infected. "We need to take off now, Sergeant," Captain Miller yelled over the firing.

"OK, here we go. Where am I going, Captain?" Sergeant Smith asked, and the chopper jolted into the air.

"Eagle One to base. Come in. I say again, Eagle One to base. Come in," Sergeant Smith said over the radio. "There is no answer, sir."

When Sergeant Smith landed the helicopter, a private came out to meet Captain Miller and his men.

"Where is the general, Private?" Captain Miller asked.

"Follow me this way, sir. In here, sir."

As the captain entered the room, he saw the general briefing some of his men about a mission. The men were armed to the teeth.

"Glad to see you, Captain. Glad to see you made it," General Rhodes said.

"General Rhodes, sir, the town is overrun with infected people. The entire outpost is gone. I need to be informed on what's going on here."

Generals Rhodes, still standing and staring at the map, replied simply, "That's classified!"

"Sir, there are hundreds of people dead, military and civilians. Those responsible could be heading this way, and your only answer is it's classified?" Captain Miller said, raising his voice and slamming his hands on the desk.

"Have your men wait outside," General Rhodes said, hands on the desk and looking the captain right in the eyes, as if to say, *No more bullshit.*

"Sergeant Smith, wait outside. I'll be fine," Captain Miller said, staring directly back at the general.

"Yes, sir. Everyone, out!" Sergeant Smith yelled.

"Everything I'm about to tell is off the record. All this started two weeks ago. The government had some kind of new drug that was supposed to cure the flu forever, and they needed to test it. So, we got a town that had a low population to test it on. We came in with some scientist who told everyone that this new vaccine would cure the flu. We gave it to everyone except the children," General Rhodes said, briefing the captain.

"You all lied to them. For what reason?" Captain Miller asked, his face turning red with anger.

"If we told them the truth, they wouldn't have taken it. And we didn't know what the side effects were. We thought we had it controlled. Well, the first week seemed to go fine, with no side effects. But then we got some reports of people acting funny. Then they died, about half the town. We put the bodies in the morgue and planned to burn it to the ground. The next day, we lost all communication with the town. So, we quarantined the area and sent some men in. We got some reports of people running around everywhere and killing everything and that these *things* would not go down. About ten minutes later, this was all we got. Listen," the general said, before pushing a button to play back a recording.

Screaming filled the room. Then after the sound of a crackling radio, a voice said, "Holy shit. Command, you there?" Then the soldier making the report was yelling. "There's one. Fire!" Shots rang out in the background, and the speaker narrated as another of the soldiers fired a whole clip into the chest and stomach of the infected. "His body," the soldier cried. "It looks like Swiss cheese, and his guts and part of his rib bones are showing. Oh my God, he's getting back up." There was silence, and then the soldier yelled again. "Keep firing, damn it. They're not going down. Get back to the hummers now." More screaming could be heard before the recording abruptly stopped.

"That's why I called you and the sergeant in. You're the best at recon, and now here you are," the general said.

"You sent us in although you knew what really happened. You're fucking dog meat. People are going to know about this. I'm going to tell them," Captain Miller yelled.

"You might not have to. We have been getting reports of some of the same symptoms that we recorded here in Dallas," General Rhodes said.

"You need to let them know what's going on so this does not happen again, you hear me?" Captain Miller said with clinched fists.

The panicked voice of a soldier came over the intercom. "General, sir."

"What is it, Private? I'm busy."

"We have a breach in the perimeter, sir!"

"Get everyone to their station now. Fire at anything that moves, you get me?" the general yelled.

"Yes, sir. But we still have men down there, sir," the soldier replied over the intercom.

"Anything down there is a threat. Do you hear me? Kill them all," the general yelled.

Firing could be heard in the background. "They broke through the fence. Oh God."

"You stand your ground, Private. You hear me."

The radio went silent.

An alarm blared.

Sergeant Smith burst through the door. "What do you want to do, sir?"

"Get to the battle stations!" the general said.

"Sorry, General. I wasn't talking to you. I was talking to the captain. What do you want to do, sir?" Sergeant Smith said, looking right at Captain Miller.

"Get to the chopper. We need to get to Dallas right away," the captain said, grabbing his gun and gear.

"What's going on in Dallas, sir?" Sergeant Smith asked.

"I'll explain it on the way," the captain replied.

"You can't leave. You have to help defend this base," General Rhodes yelled.

"Fuck you, sir. Move out, Sergeant," Captain Miller yelled back.

"Yes, sir. I'll get Hicks and Dickson and see if Hayes wants to come," Sergeant Smith said.

As they headed down the corridor to the chopper, ten infected started running at them, blood streaming down their faces.

Captain Miller, seeing this, yelled, "Battle formation. Hicks, Dickson, down in front."

Hicks and Dickson kneeled on one knee, and the others took aim over the top of them.

"Fire."

Shots rang out, and the infected dropped, one after another. Captain Miller looked up and saw one of the soldiers in the base shoot one of the infected, who had black ooze coming from his mouth and eyes, in the head. The infected jumped back up and bit his leg. The soldier shook him off, putting round after round into his attacker's head till the brains of the infected lay in a pile of black ooze, which finally stopped it from moving. The soldier looked directly at Captain Miller, tears in his eyes. He pulled his sidearm from his holster and put it to his head, pulling the trigger.

Captain Miller turned away and continued to follow his men. "*OK move*! Let's get to the chopper now," Captain Miller yelled.

Captain Miller looked over at a security monitor and saw the general, along with some of his marines, getting overwhelmed by the infected.

"Shit is that the general? What are we going to do, Captain Miller?" Hicks asked, looking at monitor.

"Nothing we can do, Hicks. Get to the chopper. When we get to the chopper hangar, it's going to be crawling with these things. Aim for the head. If you can't hit the head, go for the legs to slow them down. If more infected come on your side than you can handle, call it out. One of us can help. Hicks, Dickson, when we get to the chopper, get on those fifties for support! You all get me?" Captain Miller barked.

"Sir, yes, sir," everyone yelled.

The squad burst out of the compound door forming a circle and heading for the helipads. "Call it out if you see them coming."

"Oh, shit," Hicks yelled. "Left side. Shit! Six infected."

"Open fire." Captain Miller raised his gun and fired at two of the closest infected, dropping both as the others did the same them.

One of the infected jumped on Dickson. Half of its cheek was gone; it looked like it had been ripped off by teeth. Captain Miller grabbed it off him, throwing it over the railing and helped Dickson off the floor. "Everyone, keep moving. Don't stop."

As Captain Miller approached the chopper, his gun clicked, the rounds spent. He pulled out his knife, hitting the nearest infected in the head. He stabbed it so hard his knife nearly went through its entire head. Pulling out the knife, he saw black ooze, not blood fly into the air.

"Right side, eight more," the sergeant yelled. "Take them down. Fire."

Sergeant Smith emptied his clip. "Reloading. Cover me," he yelled.

Hayes fired at some infected and then cut down two more who were running at the chopper. He saw that their eyes looked gray and empty, like nothing was there. Blood ran from their eyes and mouths.

"I'm going to take off now. Come in. Hurry," Sergeant Smith yelled.

"Shit, reloading," Hayes yelled.

Hicks yelled, "Get down."

As Hayes got down, Hicks shots the infected in front of him. Hayes looked back at Hicks and gave him a thumbs-up.

As the chopper took off, they looked down at the once recognizable base now swarmed with infected.

Captain Miller shook his head as he watched military men, who could have had families, killed for no reason but to keep secrets. *Someone is going to pay for this,* Captain Miller thought to himself.

The others continued to stare at the base until it was nothing but a speck.

Chapter 3
President's Decision

Chief of Staff Brian Coleman, a tall, skinny, balding man with big round glasses, loved his job and was very good at it. He had always been able to help the president with his political job, catching things before they would hit the media. He walked in the Oval Office with his wife, Brenda Coleman. Also tall and slender with big glasses, Brenda loved her husband and also the blank checks that helped leap her research forward. The only person who had a bigger blank check was Jessica Price, who she hated. But like Price, she was a highly respectable scientist.

"Mr. President, sorry to bother you. But we need you to take a look at something that my wife has on her phone," Brian said.

President John Shults was sitting behind his desk reading some reports from that day. He was a very fit man, tall, with brown eyes and hair. Many times, he had been referred to by the media as the best-looking president. He didn't believe that, but he thought he could be the fittest one for sure. Seeing Brian and Brenda walk into his office always made him sweat, because it was Brian who always seemed to bring him the bad stuff. It was OK, though, because Brian was good at his job and always stopped the bad media stories before they started.

"I got this from one of my best friends, someone I used to work with in Dallas. It's just a small hospital," Brenda said, handing over her cell phone.

"What exactly am I looking at?" John asked, interested.

"It's security footage of the morgue where a man was pronounced dead," Brenda says.

As the president watched the video on the cell phone, he saw two men working in the morgue. Then, suddenly, a body bag started to move. One of the men ran over to the bag, which was now opening, and the man in the bag grabbed him and started biting his neck. The other man ran over, trying to pull the man being attacked, who was now on the floor, free. The man from the bag then bit the second man's leg. After that, the man with the bite on his leg yelled for security. As the guards came in, they shot the man in the body bag multiple times, until a shot to the head finally stopped him from snapping and squirming for good.

"What happened to the man who was in the body bag? How did he die?" John asked, looking at Brenda.

"He was attacked by his next-door neighbor. He was bit in his neck, killing him instantly. His son fought off the neighbor and was also bit on his hand, finally killing him with a knife through the head," Brenda said, concerned.

"Can we talk to the son?"

"No. According to my friend, he got sick and died of sepsis."

"Can you get your friend on the line?"

"That's the problem, Mr. President. No one is answering anywhere at the hospital or the morgue." Brenda's face fell, and she heard her own voice cracking as she thought of her friend Mary.

"Mr. President, I would like to send a team in to investigate. There have been some media outlets suggesting Dallas has zombies attacking people, but they have all gone off line. It's like all communication there is blocked in and out. No contact with any law enforcement. Nothing," Brian said.

The president pushed a button on his desk phone, and his secretary came on the other end.

"How can I help, Mr. President?"

"I want you to get the vice president, General Rhodes, the FBI director, and my chief medical advisor here as soon as possible."

"Yes, Mr. President."

The chief medical advisor, Tom Barren, and the FBI director, James Evens, came into the office.

"Mr. President," they both said.

The president pushed the button on his phone again. "Where are the vice president and General Rhodes?" John asked his secretary.

"Mr. President, they're not here. Some staff said they left a while ago in some helicopters," said the secretary's voice over the phone.

"I want you to find out where they went now!" The president's order came out with anger in his voice.

"Yes, Mr. President," the secretary said.

With his phone in hand, he walked over to his chief medical advisor and FBI director and handed them the phone.

"What's this?" they both asked, looking down at the phone.

"Just watch it. Then we will talk," the president said.

They both sat and watched the video without saying another word, and when they were finished, they both looked at the president in horror.

"Is this real?" Tom Barren, the first to talk after the video, asked.

"I'm afraid it is," Brenda Coleman said, looking horrified.

"How do you know? My department has seen videos of this type of thing over the last few hours. But it looks like kids making videos. Who sent it to you?" the FBI director asked.

"It was from a friend who I trust and who is one of the best in her field," Brenda said, her voice cracking as she thought of her friend.

"Have either of you seen or heard of anything like this?" John asked, looking around the room.

"Like I said, we've seen some videos posted online and from some media outlets, but we deemed them as posing no real threat. We get fake zombie videos all the time. Some in my department did find it strange that lines of communication between them and some of their law enforcement contacts seemed to be blocked, but nothing we thought of as a threat," the FBI director said.

"No, I haven't seen anything like this," the chief medical advisor said.

Pacing, Brenda looked at the president. "There might be someone who knows," Brenda said, looking over to her husband. "That's Jessica Price."

"The vice president's wife? Are you sure about this?" John said.

"Yes. She has worked on weird stuff like this before. At least that's what I have heard in the science community," Brenda said.

John began acting very strange upon hearing Jessica's name. He looked down at a sheet of paper on his desk, his face going blank like a poker player trying not to show his tells. "Fine. Bring her in so I can speak with her." John sounded a little mad that Jessica was being brought in.

As everyone was talking, going over the video, and calling their departments to catch them up to speed on the meeting, Jessica was escorted in by some Secret Service men. They announced her arrival.

"Jessica, please sit. We have some questions for you," the president said, eyeing her to assess her manner and body language as she walked in and took a seat across from him. Everyone else was standing behind the president. As Jessica sat, he handed her a phone. "Please, Jessica, look at the video on the phone."

As Jessica watched the scene play out, her face never moved. Nor did she make any sign of panic. She simply watched with a stone-faced expression and then handed the phone back when she was finished.

"Have you seen anything like this before?" the president asked, still looking into her face to see her answer.

"No, not exactly like that. Some of our volunteers have had side effects but nothing like what I saw in that video," Jessica said and then stopped, waiting for a response.

The president looked at her at her closely, trying to determine whether she was lying.

"What do you mean, not exactly? What is it you do at your facility?" John asked, now really studying her.

"At my facility, we develop antibodies and help people. There's nothing like that there. We do tests on people who volunteer only. Nothing illegal. As I said, there are some side effects that can affect the mind but nothing like that." Jessica felt sweat under her arms.

"What about the black site you are personally overseeing with General Rhodes?" Brenda blurted out, and Jessica looked at her with a frown on her face. She recognized that voice in the back as belonging to Brenda Coleman. She hated Brenda. The two of them had always been rivals.

"That is a military site that I help the general with. He has his own agenda, and I know very little about what goes on there. If you want to know more, you will have to ask him directly," Jessica said, looking right at Brenda and then back to the president.

"So, a facility you help with you know nothing about?" John said, his voice now stern and sounding impatient with her.

Jessica knew her husband's power couldn't help her here, and she was starting to sweat. "There is a doctor there named Rachael Morgan. She been experimenting on people with something called Compound Z. It had some side effects that made people mentally break down but not like that. I tried to put a stop to it, but the general wanted to take it further. He set up a quarantine zone in a small town and wanted to see the compound's results. I haven't heard anything from him since," Jessica said, now sweating profusely.

"Where was this facility where you were making this compound?" the president asked in an angry tone.

"It was a small facility just outside of Dallas, Texas," Jessica said.

The president asked for a map of Texas. "Where was this facility precisely?"

She pointed to a building just outside of Dallas.

"So, what happened next?" James, the FBI director, asked.

"We need to know why we can't get communication through there. Let's send in a team first to the hospital," the president said.

"I know why you can't get any communication through," Jessica said.

Everyone turned to look at her.

"General Rhodes's men developed a device that can block all communication to any area. It was still in the testing phase, but if something went wrong, he might have used it to cover himself till he can bring it under control. He has Raven Squadron at his disposal and can use them as he sees fit," Jessica explained.

"That could explain why we haven't heard or seen from anyone. If he sent men to airports blocking planes from taking off and used this technology, drones might not even get a signal out. If it can block all forms of communication, sending troops on the ground could be the only way," James said.

The president's secretary's voice came over the intercom. "Sorry to interrupt, sir. But I found out where the general and the vice president went. They both have gone to Vaccine Laboratories," the secretary said.

"Where are Vaccine Laboratories?" the president asked.

"It's Rachael Morgan's facility, sir," Jessica said.

"Why would your husband go there?" the president asked, eyeing her.

"I have no clue," she said, starting to sweat again.

"I want you to get back to your facility. Work on something to help us here. I will talk to you later. I expect something from you in an hour," the president demanded.

"Yes, Mr. President," Jessica said, rushing out the door.

"I think she knows more than she's saying," Brian said, looking at the president.

"I agree. But we need to get some troops on the ground at this hospital, and then we will deal with whatever comes next," the president said. "Here is what I want both of you to do." He pointed to Brian and the FBI director. "I want two teams, one to visit the hospital from which Brenda's friend sent the video. The other will visit this facility where they started making Compound Z."

"Yes, sir," both replied.

"We're ready, sir. We have a team going to the hospital now. But it will take an hour until we can get a team to the facility. We were going to have Raven Squadron go, but they are on an assignment for General Rhodes like Jessica said," Brian Coleman explained shortly.

"Where did he send them?" the president asked.

"We are looking into it now, sir," Brian said.

"We are all set up, sir. Here is a video feed right to the team," the FBI director said, bringing up a video on a big screen.

As the screen came to life, a soldier in a helicopter appeared in the frame.

"Soldier, who am I speaking to?" the president asked.

"Captain Dave Craven with the United States Marines, Mr. President," the captain said.

Captain Dave Craven was a tall man. One of the youngest captains, he had brown eyes and short, black hair that he liked to style so it stood up. He'd always wanted to be a marine and had always wanted to protect the president. He thought if he became a marine, the next step was Secret Service. But this new mission right from the president himself could get him there faster.

"You've been briefed on what you're going into, Captain?"

"Yes, sir. We are ready to handle anything," the captain said. But before he could say more, the feed was cut, and the screen went to static as the helicopter crossed into Texas.

Captain Craven turned to his men. "You all have been briefed on what we are facing, and this is a search and rescue. The enemy may look like a civilian. So, heads need to be in the game," he yelled.

The helicopter landed, and the captain yelled, "Move!"

Everyone jumped out of the chopper and moved toward the rooftop door, guns drawn and alert.

"Once we get in there, I want two-person teams to sweep and clear. Private Dallas, Corporal Jacobs, take left. Sergeant Hill, Private Jones, take right. Private Cole, you're with me," Captain Craven said.

"Yes, sir," they all replied.

"Everyone, turn on your cameras. I want this sweep clean and by the numbers," Captain Craven said.

"Yes, sir, they replied.

"Hill, Jones, you're on point. Dallas, Jacobs you have the rear," Captain Craven ordered.

Hill opened the door to the roof, and Jones started inside, gun drawn. They made their way down the stairwell toward the tenth-floor security door. Captain Craven and Cole followed a short distance behind. Dallas and Jacobs waited at the top of the stairs, covering the rooftop door.

Captain Craven waved to Jacobs and Dallas to work their way down the stairs and then nodded for Hill to proceed through the security door. Hill opened the door, and Jones was the first through, followed by Hill. As Hill and Jones made their way inside, they didn't see anyone manning the security post. Craven and Cole followed Hill into the security room, Dallas and Jacobs waited at the security door. Hill and Jones swept the room.

"All clear," Hill said into the radio.

Captain Craven and Cole move into the security room with Hill and Jones, followed by Dallas and Jacobs.

"Sir, here is a map of the hospital," Jones said.

"Looks like there are two hallways on each floor until the fifth floor. That's the cafeteria. Hill and Jones, you will take left. Cole and I will take right. Dallas, Jacobs, you will remain at the security door. It remains ours at all costs. It's our only way out," Captain Craven said.

"Yes, sir," Dallas said.

"Yes, sir. Nothing will get past us," Jacob said giving Dallas a fist bump.

"Everyone know your job?" Captain said.

"Sir, yes, sir," everyone replied.

"Move out," the captain said.

As Hill opened the next security door, everyone went through, guns up and stopped as they went through the door, stunned. The scene was out of a horror movie. Blood was splayed on the walls on the floor in pools. Some limbs were on the floor as if their owners had been mauled and dragged off by wolves.

"Looks like a straight chainsaw massacre film in here," Jones said.

Hill and Jones went left, going room by room. In each, they saw the same picture as they'd found out in the halls—blood and body parts. Captain Craven and Cole, going right, saw the same—until Captain Craven and Cole made their way to the seventh floor. Entering the first room, Cole saw a woman pinned under a dresser, blood pooled around her. She was moving slightly.

"Sir, I found someone," Cole said over the radio.

Captain Craven opened the door and saw Private Cole trying to lift the dresser off the woman. "Private, step back now," the captain ordered.

"Sir, she's just stuck. Together we can lift it," Cole replied.

"Private, get the fuck back now," Captain Craven said angrily.

Private Cole stopped and stepped back from the dresser, looking at the captain and saw his face, eyes wide open.

Cole went around and saw, really for the first time, what the captain was seeing. The woman's neck was torn out, and her arm was almost torn off, hanging on by only a strand of tissue.

"Cole, put a round in her head," the captain said.

"Sir?" Cole asked, shocked.

"Did I stutter, Private?" the captain said.

"Sir, I can't. We have to save her." Cole looked down at the woman, thinking of his grandma. He remembered her bringing him cookies. She was the reason he'd joined the military. Her house had been broken into while Cole was at work. The robbers had stolen her TV and jewelry. His grandma had tried to fight back, but they'd killed her. Cole felt like he needed to get away, and joining the military was the way to get as far from home as he could get. Now, looking at this lady, he had been thinking everything had come full circle—all the running from his problems had just caught up to him, and maybe he could stop running.

"She is infected, Private. Now take your gun out and put a round into her head, *now*!" the captain said, raising his voice just enough to scare the private.

Private Cole aimed and put one round into her head, and the woman stopped moving. His eyes started to swell, but he kept himself under control.

"Next time I give an order, Private, I expect you to do it," Captain Craven said, getting into Cole's face.

"Captain, do you read me?"

"What is it, Hill?" Captain replied over the radio.

"Jones and I finished the sweep and are on the fifth floor by the cafeteria, and the doors are locked," Hill said.

"Just open it."

"That's not the only problem, sir. You might want to get down here, sir," Hill replied.

Captain Craven and Cole reached the cafeteria doors and joined up with Hill and Jones.

"What is it, Hill?" Captain Craven asked.

"The door is locked, sir. But that's not the only problem. There are people inside, and they will not open the door, sir."

"We are US Marines. You have thirty seconds to open this door, or we open it by force!" the captain yelled.

"OK, man," a voice whispered. "But hush. If you make too much noise, they will be back."

The door locks slid back with a thud. Hill and Jones entered with guns raised. They pushed the man out of the way and were followed by Craven and Private Cole.

"What the fuck happened here?" Captain Craven asked the man dressed in scrubs.

"I'm Dr. Matties. He is Dr. Page. And this is Ron, the janitor. My wife sent me a text during the day saying a patient on a floor upstairs attacked a couple of nurses and had to be restrained. A few hours later, she calls me and says there are more people attacking staff, and staff were attacking staff, and she was running." Tears rolled down his face. "I saw her running. She was attacked, but I ran. I just left her." Tears were flowing now.

Dr. Page stepped in and continued. "We were eating lunch when we heard yelling down the hall and people just running down the stairs and through the cafeteria, followed by these people who were tackling people and fighting and biting. But as you looked at the people who were doing the attacking, you could see that they were mad. Their faces and eyes where messed up somehow. And they were killing people. There was blood everywhere. Dr. Matties and I were able to fight off these creatures and saved Ron over there, and we fought our way in here. We managed to lock these doors. But if we made too much noise, they would come back, banging on the doors. We haven't heard anything in a while now."

"What the fuck is wrong with this guy?" Jones asked, pointing to Ron.

"As I said, we saved Ron here. He was bitten on his arm. We managed to stop the bleeding. He has a little infection but should be fine," Dr. Matties replied.

"We are here to look for survivors and for a Dr. Mary Smith," Captain Craven said.

"She was in the cafeteria. She ran into the kitchen with some other people fighting those things," Dr. Page said.

"Is there a way out of there?" Hill asked.

"No. My bet is they went into the cooler. That's probably the most secure spot in there if they didn't die," Dr. Page said.

"All right, listen up. Hill, Jones, you're with me. We are going to the kitchen to find the doctor. Cole, you stay here. Watch these guys. We may be coming back fast, so don't fuck this up," Captain Craven said.

"Yes, sir," they all replied.

"Hill, Jones, if anyone comes at us that looks like Page described, put them down—one shot to the head. Do not hesitate, or you will be dead. Silencers on."

Craven stepped through the door first followed by Jones and Hill. As they made their way across the cafeteria, one of the infected stood up and started running at Hill, its footsteps echoing against the floor. She put one round into its head, dropping it.

They made their way into the kitchen and saw dead bodies and blood everywhere. Three infected were pounding on the cooler door. Hill and Jones took them down quickly with three shots.

"How do we know one of these people is not the doctor?" Hill said.

Just as she said that, they heard a noise come from the cooler.

"Jones, get the cooler door," Captain Craven said.

Jones grabbed the handle. Craven and Hill had their guns up and ready. The captain gave Jones a signal, and Jones swung the door open. A security guard was on the other side, ready with a knife.

"Drop it," Hill said, gun up.

The security guard dropped the knife and slowly walked out of the cooler, followed by two other people.

"We're looking for a Dr. Mary Smith," Captain Craven said.

The security guard pointed to the woman on the right, one hand still in the air.

"I'm Dr. Mary Smith," she said.

"Ma'am, I'm Captain Craven with the United Stated Marines. We are here on the president's orders to rescue you and any other survivors we find."

As the doctor was talking, they heard a noise come from the freezer, and Jones swung the door open, gun ready. Another security guard came out, holding his arm.

"Thank you," he said.

"He's bit. Put him down now, Captain," Dr. Mary Smith said. "It spreads in the bites. Once bitten, you get a fever and then die and turn into an infected. The only thing you can do is put them out of their misery, sir."

"Man, what? I feel fine, man," the security guard said, tears flowing down his face.

"Do it," Mary said.

Captain Craven gave Hill a look; she raised her gun, putting one round into the guard's head.

The other security guard went to grab Hill in anger, and she grabbed his arm, bending it backward and bringing him to his knees.

"Stop. Listen. We put him out of his misery. He would have turned and tried to kill us all," Dr. Smith said to the other guard.

"We also need to put a round in all these people around us who died by the infected. They will come back and try to kill us," Dr. Smith said.

"Jones, Hill, get on it now," Captain Craven ordered.

They started shooting every dead body on the ground.

"When they're done, we need to get all of you out of here," Captain Craven said.

Hill stopped for a second and looked at Captain Craven. "Sir, Cole's in the other room with Ron, who was bitten. He had a fever," she reminded him.

"Shit," Jones said.

"Cole, this is Captain Craven. You need to take your gun right now and put a round into Ron's head. Do it now," the captain ordered with a stern voice.

Cole raised his weapon and pointed it at Ron's head.

"Please repeat, sir," Cole said, gun shaking.

"What the fuck are you doing?" Dr. Page said.

"The captain said he's infected. I need to put him down. Now get out of the way," Cole said, gun still shaking.

"He's fine. He just fell asleep. Put the gun down," Dr. Matties said.

As Cole and Dr. Matties were talking, Dr. Page slipped behind Cole and grabbed him from behind, knocking the gun to the floor and falling on top of him. As they wrestled for the gun, they looked up to see Ron standing with his eyes closed. As Ron opened his eyes, they were white in color, just like those of all the others who had been infected. Dr. Matties and Dr. Page jumped up from the floor, Dr. Page holding Cole's gun. They watched in disbelief as Ron jumped for Cole, who was still on the ground.

As Ron dove at him, Cole managed to get his sidearm from his holster and put three bullets in the chest of the newly infected Ron, just as Ron fell on top of him.

"See. If he was infected, he wouldn't have died that easily," Page said, shaking.

As soon as those words left his, mouth Ron lunged and bit Cole's neck. Blood squirted everywhere. Both doctors started to run toward the stairwells. Cole let out a scream, and they knew all the infected must have heard.

As everything went down, Captain Craven heard everything on the radio.

"We have to move now," the captain said.

Everyone heard Cole's scream from the other room.

Jones was the first in the room. As he tried to rip the infected off Cole, it bit his hand. Jones then put a round into the head of the infected. Finally, everyone else joined Jones, seeing Ron and Cole on the ground dead.

"Captain, you need to put a shot in Cole's head before he wakes up infected," Dr. Mary Smith said.

Hill, without hesitation, shot Cole in the head.

"I shouldn't have left him here alone," Captain Craven said, looking down at the private's body.

Suddenly, they heard screams down the hall.

"The infected are coming. We need to get out of here," Hill yelled.

"We will never outrun them," Mary said, her voice frantic, thinking she should have just stayed in the cooler.

"Give me your grenades and your extra clips. I will hold them off as long as possible," Jones said. Blood was now flowing freely from his hand.

"What the fuck are you talking about?" Hill said.

Jones lifted his hand, showing the bite, and Hill dropped her head.

"How did that happen?" Captain Craven asked, looking at his hand.

"Trying to pull the infected off Cole. There's no time to argue. Just get them out of here," Jones said, grabbing the grenades from Hill.

"You heard him. Let's move," Captain Craven yelled.

"You don't have to do this," Hill said, trying to hold back her emotions as tears wanted to come. She knew that's not what he would want.

"I'm not going to end up like one of those fucking things. I'm going out my way. Now get the fuck out of here," Jones yelled, grabbing the grenades and clips from Captain Craven.

Hill turned and ran for the stairwell. As she reached the stairs, she looked back and saw Jones firing at a herd of the infected coming at him. Hill ran up the stairs, the echoes of gunshots ringing out behind her.

Jones watched as Hill got to the stairwell. He turned around, aimed his weapon at the first horde coming toward him, and opened fire. His clipped emptied faster than he realized. As a second wave came at him, he had just enough time to fire, and his gun jammed. He grabbed the grenades he had hooked on his vest and pulled them. Just as the infected took him down, the grenades went off, killing the infected and bringing down the walls and ceiling around him.

Drs. Page and Matties got to the top floor and started walking down the hall—straight toward the drawn weapons of Jacobs and Dallas.

"Halt. Who's there? Drop your weapon now," Jacobs yelled down the hall.

Dr. Matties stopped in his tracks and threw up his hands. Page stopped, the gun still in his hands shaking.

"I'm Dr. Page. This is Dr. Matties."

"Well, Dr. Matties, why don't you tell him to lower the gun, or we will put him down?" Dallas replied, guns pointed at them both.

Dr. Page looked at Dr. Matties. "Put the gun down."

"Fuck that. They will kill us just like Ron. You know it, and I know it."

"I'm not asking again," Dallas yelled.

Dr. Page started to lower the gun, and an explosion shook the building. Startled, Dallas shot Dr. Page, and then both Dallas and Jacobs pointed their guns at Dr. Matties and walked toward him. After reaching him, Jacobs kneeled alongside Dr. Page and felt for a pulse. Recognizing the gun the doctor had been holding, he showed Dallas and grabbed Dr. Matties by the throat.

"Where the fuck did you get this gun?" Dallas yelled at him.

"We got it off a guy who tried to kill our friend Ron, man." Dr. Matties was shaking.

"Where is the rest of the team? And what was that fucking explosion?" Jacobs asked, pointing his gun at Dr. Matties.

Just then, Captain Craven and the others appeared, everyone running toward the checkpoint.

"What the hell is going on? We heard shots, and it sounded like an explosion?" Dallas said.

As the others ran down the hall, Hill saw Dr. Matties and stopped.

"You motherfucker," she said, grabbing Matties.

"What's going on?" Dallas asked.

"This motherfucker killed Cole and got Jones fucking killed," Hill yelled back, still trying to grab Matties as Jacobs held her back.

"We don't have time for this, Captain," Mary yelled.

"She is right. We need to get to the chopper and get out of here before we get overrun," Captain Craven said.

"Overrun by what?" Jacob asked.

"By infected," Mary Smith yelled, running down the hall toward the roof.

"Infected?" Dallas yelled back.

"Get to the roof door!" Captain Craven was yelling for Hill and Dallas to get the hell out.

But they remained standing by Matties. They gave each other a look.

"You guys aren't going to kill me, are you?" Matties asked, shaking.

"No. All you have to do is hold off the infected so we can grab our gear, and we will be even," Hill said.

"All right, what do you want me to do?" Matties said, relaxing for a second.

Hill turned around and shot Matties in both knees. As he fell to the ground crying, Dallas ran for the roof door. He looked back and saw tons of infected by the stairwell door. "Let's move," he called to Hill.

"That's for Cole and Jones, bitch," Hill said, walking away from Matties.

Hill and Dallas finally got on the chopper with everyone else.

"Where is Dr. Matties?" Captain Craven yelled at Hill and Dallas as the chopper took off.

"He didn't make it," Hill said, looking out the chopper, never meeting the captain's eyes.

The pilot handed a sat phone to Captain Craven as they left Texas and signal returned. "It's the president, sir. He wants to talk to Dr. Mary," the pilot said.

Mary took the phone. "Yes, Mr. President."

"After dealing with these infected, is there anything you recommend we do, Mary?" the president asked.

"We need to quarantine the entire state of Texas now—no one in, no one out at all costs. Containment is the only answer until we can find a way to deal with this," Mary said.

"Thank you, Mary. Let me talk to the captain," the president said.

"Captain, I want you on the ground leading this. No one gets out. If they do and they're infected, this could go beyond our control. I'm activating Code Raven. Use that for all commanders. They know what it means. President out."

As Jessica was leaving, she was met by two Secret Service men. "Ma'am, come with us."

Jessica looked annoyed, but she did follow the agents. They led her to a door that looked as if it had appeared out of nowhere. One of the men opened it with a card and told her to have a seat. As she walked into the room, she saw it had two-way glass, and the thought occurred to her that this was where they interrogated people. As she took a seat, the president came in through another door on the far side of the room and sat across from her. "I'm taking a risk here, Jessica, talking to you. You told me that General Rhodes had this quarantined, only for me to find out from one of my staff about an outbreak." The president was straight-faced and staring right at her.

"I thought he had. Now you've sent a team to search for a scientist and brought a lot of people into the loop who didn't need to be. What will you do now, sir?" Jessica said.

"I had to. I had to maintain that I knew nothing. These people can either be bought or dealt with. Captain Craven is loyal and expendable. What I want to know is what General Rhodes has done to try and clean his end up," John said.

"He sent a Navy SEAL he trusted. I believe his name was Captain Miller, along with two men from the Raven Squadron to keep an eye on them," Jessica replied.

"Well, now I have to clean it up—his and your mess—and possibly kill thousands because you fucked up. I will handle my end. You go back to your facility and find us something that can help us here. Once you do, I will send the vice president to help. My men will see you out," John said.

As she got up to walk out, the president grabbed her wrist. "Just so you know, you can be replaced," John said as Jessica pulled her arm from his grip.

"Are you threatening me?" Jessica said, looking at him.

"No. I don't threaten. Just remember that," John replied as Jessica walked out.

Chapter 4

The Quarantine

Texas Border outside Gainesville

Kyle never really wanted to be in the military. But he did meet his wife here, and she lived in Iowa. She got out last year. He had one more year, and they had a daughter. He thought he would be sent out to Germany, but his hole platoon had been sent here, along with tons of others and the National Guard. They were told they were to have no contact with their family or friends, and no one was to leave Texas—something about an infection. But he never pictured these men at guard at nights with orders to shoot to kill anyone attempting to escape. Every so often, someone would approach with a wound that looked like bite marks and would be taken away and never seen again. He was sick of it, and his thoughts were of his family because he was scared. He saw a man approach and one of the other guards walk up to him.

"Get back to your car, sir," the soldier said.

"Fuck that. My family needs out of here. We know what is coming. Let us pass," the man, who Kyle would learn was Stan, yelled back.

The soldier pushed Stan hard, knocking him to the ground, and he landed on his ass, the soldier standing over him. Private Kyle, pulled on the other soldier's arm as the soldier kicked Stan in the chest. "That's enough," Kyle said, helping Stan to his feet.

"This is bullshit. I'm an American, and I pay taxes. I pay your fucking salary," Stan yelled.

"Sir, please go back to your family. We are here to help. Once we have information, we will let you know," Kyle said.

"Yeah, I can tell you're here to help," Stan said, walking back to his car and family.

Sergeant Davis walked over to the men, having seen the whole thing. "Is everything all right?" the sergeant asked.

"Yes, sir," both of the soldiers said.

"Carry on then."

Sergeant Davis started to walk away.

"Sir, when are we going to start the evacuation? If the things we've seen on the videos are real, those things are coming, and there are families everywhere," Kyle said.

"Our orders, Private, are to hold this position at all costs—no one in, no one out. So, that's what we're going to do. Got that, Private?" the sergeant said.

"Sir, and what if those civilians come across running or driving? What are we supposed to do, sir?" Kyle asked.

The sergeant turned around and grabbed Kyle. "Listen up. As you said, we know what's coming. And if any of them are infected, we could lose everything. I have family in Oklahoma. How about you?" the sergeant asked.

"I have a wife and a kid, sir, in Iowa, sir."

"And would you kill every single person on that other side to keep them safe, because I know I would?" the sergeant said.

"Yes. I would do anything to protect my family. But we're talking about killing innocent people, who are just scared. You think everyone will open fire when the captain gives that order?" Kyle replied.

"Well let's hope we don't have to find out. Now, back to your post, *Private*!" the sergeant replied.

Stan walked back to his car and family, getting angrier by the minute. No one talked to him like that. He paid their salaries. He was going to show them. Stan had always been the popular one—the star running back in high school. But now, his muscles had started to get flabby, he had a gut, and he was even losing his hair. When all this started, he had been at work. His wife had called to say the neighbors were leaving because of things they'd heard about riots in the city and people getting killed. So, Stan and Kelly were going to do the same thing. When they stopped for gas, they were attacked, and their daughter was bitten. When she died and changed, they couldn't put her down like so many people they'd run into had had to do with family members or friends. They'd decided to tie her up and hope there would be a cure. Stan was going to get them out of here because he had a plan.

All the other people were waiting for Stan by all the cars.

"What did the soldiers say?" Kelly, his wife, asked.

"They're not going to let anyone pass," Stan said.

"What does that mean? Don't they know what's coming?" Frank, a man from another car, asked.

Everyone started yelling and screaming at each other, and a few fights started.

Stan finally spoke out above the rest. "I have a plan. Just go back to your cars and families, and we will meet in one hour," he yelled.

"You have a plan? Our daughter needs help now. There has to be a cure, something they're not telling us. We need to get through for her," Kelly yelled at him.

"Don't you think I know that? Just stay by the car. I'm going to talk to the other guys here."

As Stan walked away, one of the wives walked up to Kelly. "Our daughter was wondering if Rebecca can come and play," she asked.

"I'm sorry. She is sleeping. Maybe later," Kelly replied.

Kelly walked up and looked in her car at Rebecca in the back seat. Her daughter was tied up, and her mouth was gagged and taped. She was squirming around in the back seat. Both Stan and Kelly had known she was infected when they saw it happen. They just hoped there was a cure for her somewhere.

Stan walked up to the other guys in other cars.

"What's your plan?" one of the guys asked.

"Tomorrow at dawn, we're going to drive right through that barricade and keep driving," Stan said.

"That's your big plan? They're going to kill you," another guy said.

"They're not going to kill us. We're unarmed civilians. At the most, we will be arrested and detained. And if we're on the other side and safe, and—who knows?—if enough of us get passed, maybe they will just not do nothing. They may just think it's too much to round up scared people," Stan said.

"If this is going to work, we will need a lot of us. I have my CB radio, and it's working. I've been talking to another group a few miles away, and they're mad. I can talk to them and see if they want to go," one of the guys said.

"Perfect. They could give us a chance. Tell whoever is in to go at dawn when the sun is just coming up—around six. And we will do the same. Who's with me?" Stan said.

Almost all the men in the group agreed.

Just before dawn, Stan started his engine, and a lot of others did as well. He looked at his watch and put his hand out the window and made a circular gesture to say, *Let's go.*

"I hope you know what you're doing," Kelly said.

Stan looked at her and jammed the car into gear.

Kyle was on the morning shift; he hated the morning shift. Nothing was ever going on this early. Just as he thought that, a car crashed through the barricade, almost hitting him as he jumped away. As he turned to look, he saw it was the guy from yesterday who had asked to pass. *I think his name was Stan*, he recalled.

Alarms everywhere started to wail, and the sergeant ran out of his office.

"Stop those cars. Live fire is authorized. Fire!" he yelled.

Stan in the lead car got by the other checkpoint easily, followed by two cars. Kelly looked back to see Carl and Stephanie trying to pass the first barricade. Their car was swarmed and then hit by a hail of bullets. She gasped.

"Carl and Stephanie's car just got shot up. They had five kids in there. I thought you said they wouldn't shoot unarmed civilians. I told you this was a bad idea," Kelly yelled.

Stan stepped on the gas even harder as he looked in the mirror and saw the military chasing them with vehicles and a helicopter. He looked at the family in the car next to him, recalling the father's name was Barry. Barry started to slow down and then came to a stop. Stan kept watching the rearview mirror, and Kelly was looking out the back, window. So, both saw Barry stop and saw that the officers at the military checkpoint they'd blown through didn't even get out to arrest them. They just opened fire.

"They were trying to surrender. You didn't have to shoot," Kyle yelled from one of the Humvees.

"We have our orders, Private," one of the soldiers yelled back.

"There were fucking kids in there," Kyle yelled back.

The sergeant pulled up. "All right, let's get the other two," the sergeant said.

"Sir, there are families in those cars. They're just scared," Kyle said.

"They could be infected, and we can't let it get out, Private. Now move now," the sergeant replied.

Stan saw the other car try to turn and go a different way. The car exploded, shot by the helicopter following them.

"What are we going to do, Stan?" Kelly yelled.

Kelly looked in the back seat and saw that Rebecca's gag had come off, and she was awake and squirming. "Stan, Rebecca's awake, and she is squirming," she said.

Just then, Stan saw a rocket fly from a helicopter and flip the car. Stan was dazed for a second. He looked over to Kelly and saw Rebecca biting her neck. Screaming, he got out of the car as fast as possible. The Humvees pulled up.

"Help my wife. It's our daughter, Rebecca; she's sick. Please help," Stan yelled.

The men got out of the vehicle, and pushed Stan to the ground, guns drawn on him. The sergeant got out and walked around to the passenger side.

"Bring Private Kyle here now," he yelled.

Kyle walked over, and the sergeant told the men to drag the little girl and the woman out of the car. Kyle looked down at the little girl, who was still snapping her jaws, trying to get more flesh.

"You see, Private. This could have been the situation in those other vehicles. This infected just killed her mom, and now it will grow. She will become infected. So, what I want you to do, Private, is put a round in both of their heads," the sergeant said.

"What?" Kyle said.

"That's the only way to put an infected down."

"She's just hurt, sir. She needs help," Kyle replied.

The sergeant took out his gun, shooting the little girl in the chest. "Does she still need help, Private? She's still moving."

Rebecca kept squirming as Kyle looked on in horror, not believing what he was seeing.

"Now put a round in her head, or I will put a round in yours," the sergeant said.

Kyle lifted his gun, shaking, and fired one shot into Rebecca's head. She stopped squirming.

"Now the mom," the sergeant said.

"Sir, she's dead," Kyle replied.

"Yes, and she was infected by the bite. So put her down now. If she gets up and turns, she could infect us all," the sergeant said.

Again, he pointed his gun. As he did so, her eyes popped open, startling him, and she jumped to her feet, launching herself onto the soldier right next to her and biting his neck. All the soldiers opened fire, killing them both.

The sergeant grabbed Kyle. "Look here, motherfucker. Next time, you'd better follow my fucking orders. We just lost a man because of your chicken-shit everyone-deserves-a-chance shit. This is what the infected do. Now go around the front and take care of the man," the sergeant said.

Kyle walked around to the front of the vehicle and saw Stan there crying. Looking at him, Kyle raised his gun. This time, he fired without hesitation, putting a round into his head and dropping him.

"I want all the bodies put together and burned now, along with all the cars. Make sure everyone who was shot has a round to the head. Move now, people," the sergeant yelled.

Back in the Oval Office, the chief of staff showed the president some footage from the shooting at the checkpoint.

"This has happened at all the checkpoints, sir. Hundreds of citizens are dead, some infected, others trying to bring infected across the border for help. But we can't cover something this big up. The people who survive in these blockades will speak out. And you will go down as the guy who let this happen," the chief of staff said.

"Sorry, sir, to bother you," the president's secretary cut in. "Mr. President, you told me to let you know as soon as I heard. Well, the Raven Squadron was sent to the airport in Dallas, and the vice president went to his wife's facility in Dallas. We don't know why," she said.

The president looked at the chief of staff. "Send the squad to the airport to see what's going on. And have the head of Raven Squadron meet us at this quarantined area. I want to see this for myself."

"Who do we send to the other facility, sir?" Brian asked.

"Who's that captain that helped us at the hospital?" the president asked.

"That was Captain Craven, sir. You sent him to set up the barricades around Dallas," Brian said.

"Send him and whatever squad he has left to retrieve this formula," the president said.

"What about the vice president and the doctor, Rachael?" Brian asked.

"Find them at all costs. We need a cure if they have one," the president said.

"What about all the surviving people at the barricades? What do you want us to do with them?" Brian asked.

"Have the soldiers round everyone up. We're not sure who's infected and who's not. We will see if this cure works," the president said.

"Wait a minute. You can't just round everyone up. I just told you there might be a cure. We need to find this out before we go about exterminating everyone," the chief medical advisor said.

"That's right. There *might* be a cure. There might not. We can't risk it. In less than seventy-two hours, this virus has killed an entire state. If it gets out, it could kill millions more. We can't risk this on a maybe. So, we round everyone up and kill anyone who turns. We will see if this cure works," the president said.

"Yes, sir," she said, head down.

"So, it's settled. Get ahold of Captain Craven and tell him he's my new Raven Squadron," the president said, smiling.

Chapter 5

Chaos Spreads

Dallas, Texas

Dr. Steve Bradley was a very handsome man with blond hair and blue eyes. He had always believed in science before everything—until he'd met his wife. He had been in the military serving as a scientist at the time, and he couldn't use science to find out what made him feel love at first sight. He'd volunteered to join Rachael Morgan's research team with his wife. The team was researching a new vaccine that could not just cure the cold but also help fight all viruses. He'd been sent to a town to collect data on the vaccine and had already been given something called Compound V. Then he got news that his wife had fallen ill and that he needed to get back to her. So he was given the samples to take back to the facility by Nancy, but his thoughts were on his wife.

"This sucks, doesn't it, Doc? You and I are driving some classified documents to a scientist for some crazy project that's an hour and a half away. What are the odds, a private with a doctor?" Jackson said.

Private Dezmond Jackson was a young black man. He joined the military to be a pilot. He'd been flying his dad's helicopters since he was sixteen helping where he could. He wanted to fly choppers while in the military. Before he was shipped off, he was ordered to bring Dr. Bradley wherever he needed to go. It wasn't what he wanted, but he'd never been one to turn away from an order.

Bradley was preoccupied with his thoughts about his wife. He just turned to the soldier and said, "Yep."

The private continued to ramble on about stuff Bradley wasn't interested in.

"Private, stop!" Bradley yelled suddenly.

"What the hell is that?" Jackson said.

Squinting, Bradley made out a young lady running at them, arms flailing back and forth and yelling at them to stop. As they got closer, they could see she was crying.

Both men get out of the Jeep to confront the panicked woman, who was trying to catch her breath and still crying.

"Ma'am, are you all right?" Bradley asked.

"What's chasing you? And where is it?" Jackson asked.

"There!" She pointed to a deformed figure running at them from a distance.

"Get behind me," Jackson said, drawing his weapon. "Sir, stop and put your hands on your head! Do it *now*, or I will fire on you!"

As the figure got closer, they could see that the running man was very pale and had lots of blood on his shirt. As he drew closer still, they saw blood around his mouth and what looked like blood oozing from his eyes.

The private put one round into the man's leg, making the man stumble and fall. But he got right back up and continued toward them.

"Put him down now," Bradley yelled.

Jackson put two rounds in the man's chest, dropping him. As he turned to find out if the woman and Bradley were OK, the woman shrieked. And Jackson turned around to see the man again rise to his feet. Again, he put two more rounds into him, still not stopping him. Jackson then aimed at the oncoming figure's head and fired, dropping him this time. He held his gun on the man to see if he got back up. After he didn't, Bradley walked over, being cautious. Looking at the man, he saw a gash and what seemed to be a missing chunk around his neck. He turned back to the woman. "Are you OK?" he asked.

"Well kind of. I saw him before. He helped pump gas at a station not too far from here. I walked back to this station when my car was broken down. I tried calling someone but couldn't get a signal for some reason. As I was walking to the door, he jumped out from behind me and bit my arm. I barely got away." The woman's voice shook with fear as she told her story, tears still in her eyes.

"Private, get on the radio and tell the command we're heading back," Bradley said with a little panic in his voice.

"Ma'am, you're going to be OK. Can I take a look at your arm?" Bradley reached for her arm.

The woman showed him her arm. Bradley looked at it and saw it already looked infected, even as blood still dripped from her wound. Bradley went to the back of the jeep and grabbed what little first aid kit it had on board. Wrapping her arm, he told her to get into the back of the jeep and helped her in.

"Doc, there's nothing. It's like we've been disconnected," Jackson said.

"We need to get her back to the base as quickly as possible," Bradley said, looking at Jackson with a look of fear.

"Doc, is there something going on you're not telling me? I have a bad feeling about this," Jackson said.

Bradley leaned into whisper. "Private, I'm not entirely sure. It looks bad, and if she was bitten and he had some kind of disease, he might have given it to her. So we need to move now if we're going to save her life."

"Yes, sir, Doc," Jackson said.

"Ma'am, just lie down. We will be there in no time," Bradley said.

After Jackson had been driving for a bit, he looked back at the woman and looked at Bradley. "She doesn't look so good, Doc," he said.

Bradley looked in the back. After taking the woman's pulse, he said simply, "You might want to step on it, Private."

"Base, this is Private Jackson. Can anyone respond? I repeat. This is Private Jackson. Is anyone there?" Jackson said, again trying the radio as they got closer to the base.

"There's the base, sir. What the hell's going on here?" Jackson said. Looking around, he surmised that everyone had left in a hurry, leaving anything they couldn't carry on the ground.

"I don't know, Private," Bradley replied as he took in the scene. "Go check the rooms for anyone. Here's your rifle. Be careful. Keep your eyes open. Here's a radio. Stay in touch. I will check these building down here."

Before, the base had been active, occupied by an entire squad. Now, it looked like a ghost town.

Jackson returned to meet up with Bradley after looking at some of the buildings upstairs.

"You find anything, Private?"

"No, sir. But it looks like they left in a hurry," Jackson replied.

"Let's get back to the Jeep ASAP. We're going into town to find out what's going on," Bradley said.

With that, he and Jackson turned to the Jeep. Jackson spoke up first. "Doc, where's the girl? She was right there. What the fuck is going on?" Jackson looked around the jeep to see if she had fallen.

The sound of footsteps comes from a tent to the right.

"Show yourself, or I will fire on you," Jackson yelled, his voice trembling and nervous.

"*Stop*! It's me," Corporal Huston yelled back.

"What are you doing, Corporal?" Bradley let out a sigh of relief.

"Well, there was an alarm telling us to evacuate, and then some choppers came and started picking us up. Me and twenty others didn't get on. The others moved out on foot. I said I was waiting for another chopper. But none came, so here I am," Huston said.

"You haven't seen a girl around, have you? She was in our back seat. Now she's missing," Jackson said.

"Nope. Sure haven't. But let's get the hell out of here, if that's OK with you, Bradley," the corporal said.

As the corporal started to walk to the jeep, the girl jumped on him, biting his neck. He screamed. Jackson fired a round into her head.

"What the fuck is going on?" Jackson said, his voice sounding panicked.

"Corporal, you all right?" Bradley leaned down and checked the corporal's pulse.

"He's dead, isn't he? What's going on here?"

As Jackson was talking, the corporal jumped to his feet.

"Are you all right, Corporal?" Jackson yelled as he raised his gun.

Just then, the corporal screamed and ran at Bradley. Jackson put two rounds in his chest, but he kept coming. Just before he reached Bradley, Jackson shoulder-checked him to the ground, putting one round in his head.

"What do you think is going on, sir? This is crazy. Have you heard of anything like this?" Jackson asked, looking right at Bradley.

"I don't know. We need to get to the facility where my wife works, where we were headed. Rachael's a brilliant scientist. If anyone knows anything, it would be her," Bradley said.

A sound started coming from a tent. "Jackson, what the hell is that?" Bradley asked.

"It's coming from that tent, sir," Jackson replied.

A radio in the tent crackled to life. "This is Eagle One. Come in, Echo Base. I repeat, this is Eagle One. Is anyone there?"

"Yes, Eagle One. This is Private Jackson. I read you."

"This is Captain Miller with Special Forces. Who's your commanding officer, Private. I need to speak with him."

"It's just me and Dr. Bradley," Jackson said.

"All right, Private. We will be landing in five minutes. Please stand by," Captain Miller replied.

"Yes, Captain," Jackson replied. "Over and out."

"Why are we going to Dallas Echo Base?" the sergeant questioned.

"Sergeant, the general briefed me that there were reported signs of the same symptoms as what we saw in the town. If that's true, things are going to be getting out of hand. And people have a right to know what's going on. But our priority is to find your son, Sergeant," Captain Miller said, putting his hand on the sergeant's shoulder.

"Thank you, Captain."

Jackson looked in the sky and soon saw the approaching chopper. "Here they come," he said, pointing.

"How many are there, Jackson?"

"Looks like five."

"Captain, this base is supposed to be pretty big right, sir?" Dickson said, looking out the chopper at the base.

"Yes. Why, Dickson?" Captain Miller replied.

"Because there's nobody down there, sir, that I can see."

"Maybe they're all at lunch," joked Hicks.

The sergeant gave the captain a concerned look as they came into land. As they landed, Bradley was there to meet them.

"Hello, Dr. Bradley," Captain Miller said, offer his hand.

Shaking Miller's hand, Bradley replied, "Hello, Captain. This is Private Jackson. And I'm Dr. Bradley."

"Where is everyone?" Captain Miller asked, glancing around the deserted-looking base and then back at the sergeant.

"I don't know, Captain. We just retuned and found this base empty as well. The corporal over there told us the base had been evacuated," Jackson said, pointing to the body on the floor.

"What? After he told you, you shot him?" Hicks said jokingly.

The captain walked over and looked at the corpse of the lady and the corporal. Noticing the bites on his neck and her arm, he looked back at the sergeant. "Same as Johnson and Rodriguez," he said as he stood up.

"You know something about this, Captain?" Bradley asked.

"Possibly. Why don't you tell me what you know?" Captain Miller said. Looking into the Jeep the private and the doctor had come, he took note of the seal on the package they were carrying.

"I can't tell you anything, Captain. It's classified," Bradley said.

"There's that word again. I can't stand it. *Classified.* If you want our help, you need to tell us what's going on. Or you can stay here and die. I don't care," Captain Miller said, staring Bradley right in the face.

"You know what's going on? And you didn't say anything?" Jackson said looking angrily at Bradley.

"Bring me to the Acylate facility, and you will find out everything. I promise," Bradley replied.

"Sorry, Doc. First, we need to find my sergeant's kid. I promised him. So, we will help after we find him. Help us, so we can help you," Captain Miller said.

"His son? I think there are bigger problems here, Captain."

"Fuck you," the sergeant said, grabbing Bradley. "He's the only thing I have left in this in this world. I promised him I would be back."

The captain yelled at the sergeant to back down.

The sergeant let him go and went to sit by the jeep, recalling the day before he left on this mission—the one he wasn't going to go on.

"Dad, you promised. You told me you would be here this week. You told me after your last mission that was it. This isn't fair." Tom was crying as he hugged his dad.

"I had a friend ask for me specifically to do this mission, and I owe him," the sergeant had explained. "I will be done after this one. Have I ever not returned from a mission? I always come back." Looking down at his son's face, he'd given him one more hug before grabbing his gear and walking out of the room. "I'll be back before you know it." He'd given Tom a wink while walking out. Now he wished he would have stayed.

"Fine. Captain, I need your help. But I don't know what I can do to help you," Bradley said.

"You can drive, can't you?" Captain Miller asked.

Bradley nodded.

"All right. Hayes, Hicks, look through the base and find us some wheels," the captain said.

"Yes, sir," Hicks and Hayes replied.

"Found some, sir," Hicks yelled, driving up in a Hummer.

"I'll have Private Jackson drive one. Bradley, you got the other," the captain said.

"Hicks, get in Bradley's Hummer and get on the fifty cal. Dickson, you're on the other fifty," Captain Miller said.

"Sir, why do Hicks and I always have to be on the guns?" Dickson asked.

"Because you are the best riflemen we have, and because I said so," Captain Miller said.

"Yes, sir," Dickson replied.

"Sergeant, you're with me," the captain said.

"Yes, Captain. Let's move," Bradley said, a little annoyed.

"OK, Sergeant. Where we headed?"

"When we get into town, Captain, we have to go down one of the main streets. And if there's a lot of infected people, it could get hairy, sir," Sergeant Smith said.

As they turned the corner onto the main street, they saw hundreds of people running, screaming, and fighting the infected. As they drove, people screamed for them to stop and help. One man jumped on the back of the hummer Bradley was driving. Hicks panicked and shot him. His first few shots ripped through the man's arm, blowing it apart and sending blood and bone flying. His second round of shots hit the man in the chest, ripping through him like butter. His body flew off the Hummer and hit the ground, lying in the road, nearly cut in half, blood pooling under him.

Bradley, seeing this through the rearview mirror, yelled, "Hicks, what the fuck are you doing?"

"He could have been infected."

"Bradley, Hicks is right. All these people are now a threat. We don't know who has been infected or not."

"Hicks, Dickson, anyone goes for the Hummer, kill them. You got me," the captain yelled over the radio.

"Yes, sir," Hicks and Dickson replied in unison.

"Holy shit, man. Look at all these people. This is nuts, man!" Private Jackson said.

"Calm down, Jackson. Keep your cool. Keep going. Don't stop for anything or anyone. If we do, we could get swarmed," the captain said.

"Yes, sir," Jackson replied.

Three more people started running at the Hummers, screaming for help, Hicks shot at them. The rounds took off limbs and stopped the pursuers in their tracks as they fell dead in the street.

A girl jumped in front of the Hummers. Jackson, driving the lead Hummer, pushed on the gas and closed his eyes. He hit her straight on. Her body exploded and blood flew up into Dickson's face. Wiping his face, he saw not just blood but also brain matter. He leaned over the side of the Hummer and puked. "What the fuck, man?" Dickson tried to say as he puked again.

"What the hell is wrong with you, Dickson?" Captain Miller yelled seeing him puke.

"Sorry, Captain. Jackson hit a woman," Dickson replied, puking again.

The Hummers turned down the next street, leaving the people chasing them in the dust. Bradley watched in the rearview mirror as they fell behind.

"Wait!" Hayes said over the radio, making the private stop the Hummer.

"Why did we stop?" the captain asked.

"Think about it. If we're on a rescue mission, you don't go announcing that you're coming. If there are a lot of infected there, we might as well not blow a horn. We're going to need to go in stealth-like."

"Hayes is right. We're going to have to go in silent, if we want to save the sergeant's kid," the captain agreed.

"All right. What we need is a plan," the sergeant said.

"OK. This what we're going to do. Hicks, Dickson, Sergeant Smith, and I will get our night gear and some silencers and get the sergeant's kid. Jackson, Hayes, and Bradley will stay with the Hummers. We will radio you for pickup when we're ready," the captain said.

"Sounds like a plan."

"Let Jackson know when we get two blocks away, Sergeant," the captain instructed.

"Yes, sir," the sergeant said and then, a few minutes later, noted, "We're here, sir."

"Captain, good luck," Bradley said.

"Thanks, sir. All right, men, move out. We've all been on missions before. We know what to do. Hicks, take point."

"Yes, sir."

When the extraction team had made it to the end of the block, the captain checked the comms. "You still read us, Hayes?"

"Yes, Captain. Loud and clear."

"*Hold*!"

"What is it, Hicks?"

"Captain, we got three bogies about half a block down. Looks like they're eating something!"

"All right, on my go, take them down. Remember to aim for the head. Three, two, one, take them down."

The rifles whispered in the night air.

"All three down, sir!"

"Good work. Keep moving, Hicks."

"Yes, sir."

When the team had just one more block to go, screaming suddenly echoed across the open parking lot before them.

"What the hell is that, Captain?"

"Not sure. Everyone, down. Dickson you see anything?"

"Not yet." In the distance, he spotted a girl running and screaming. "Sir, it's a woman. She may need help."

"Stay where you are, Dickson. You know our mission."

"Captain, she will die!"

"Stay put."

"*Fuck it*!"

"Dickson, *get back here now*!

"God damn it. Go help him."

More shots whispered through the air.

"Take them down," the captain instructed.

Hicks, Captain Miller, Dickson and Sergeant Smith started taking down the infected running after the woman.

"Cease fire."

The sergeant grabbed Dickson. "This better not fuck the mission, or you're dead. Next time Captain says stay put, you stay put, motherfucker."

"Sorry. I just couldn't stand to watch her get killed. Lady! Are you hurt? Can you understand me?"

"Man, that bitch is fucking scared out of her mind, Captain."

"Shut it, Hicks."

"Lady, are you hurt?"

"No, I am fine."

"Are you bit?"

"No."

"Captain, we can't take here with us. She's too much of a risk."

"I said shut it, Hicks."

"Sir, Hicks is right. She could be bit, and she could be lying."

"Lady, what I need you to do right now—and I mean right now; there's not much time—is strip down naked. We need to see if you are bitten."

"What? No. I won't!"

"It's either that or get left here. It's your choice, lady."

"Fine," the lady says, annoyed and strips down.

Hicks checked her for bites. "Yes, sir. She's clean."

"OK. Get dressed. We need to keep moving. Dickson, you saved her. She's your baggage. Got me?"

"Yes, Captain."

"All right. Hicks, you're on point. Move out."

"Move out, yes, sir.

They'd moved just half a block ahead when Hicks yelled, "Hold!"

"What is it, Hicks?"

"We got two in front of the building."

"Sir, what if they're not infected?

"Shut it, Dickson. Your shit almost got us killed before. We're taking them out. Hicks, remember, aim for head."

"Yes, sir." Hicks shot both targets in the head. "Targets down, sir."

"Move up. Sergeant, what floor are we going to?"

"Fifth floor, Captain."

"All right listen up. Once we're in there, weapons free. Everything is a target, infected or not, until we get to the sergeant's son. Anyone have a problem with that?"

"*No, sir!*"

"Lady, I need you to keep up and keep quiet. Move out."

Hicks knocked on the door the sergeant indicated and then opened it slowly.

The captain moved up. "Checks those corners, Hicks."

They moved through the lobby.

"Stairs here," Hicks said pointing at the stairs.

"Heading to the second floor!" the captain said over the radio.

"Good, Captain. We will be ready to pick up. Standing by."

"Sergeant, what floor?"

"Fourth floor, sir."

Hicks kept moving. On the third floor, he held up hand, "Hold!"

"What is it, Hicks?"

"Two infected. Wait. There are three. Takedowns, sir?"

"Yes, on my mark. Go."

The captain and Hicks took them down quickly.

Hicks opens the fourth-floor stairwell door.

"Check those corners and keeps moving. Sergeant, what is the room number?"

"It's 429, just down the hall."

Hicks signaled to stop. "Here. I found the room."

"All right, Sergeant. Get on my ass."

"Dickson, remain outside with the lady to make sure she stays quiet and nothing happens. We may need to get out quickly."

"Yes, sir."

Hicks opened the door; he grabbed his mouth as he gagged.

"What is it, Hicks?" the captain asked.

"Are you sure he's still alive? There is a lot of blood here!"

The sergeant fell to his knees. Finding his son's ball cap on the ground, he started to cry. "God damn it. I wasn't fast enough!"

They heard a noise in the back hallway.

"What the fuck is that?"

The sergeant followed as the others headed down the hall. A figure jumped out, its face half eaten. Hicks took it down.

The sergeant looked down at the body and yelled, "That's my mom. What the fuck?" Grabbing Hicks, he wrapped his hands around the corporal's throat, slamming him against the wall. The captain grabbed the sergeant around his throat, pulling him off Hicks. The sergeant dropped to his knees, crying over her body.

"Sergeant, look at her face. She was one of them. She was not your mom anymore. She was infected. She would have killed all of us. You know that. I'm sorry," Captain Miller said, grabbing the sergeant's shoulder.

The sergeant got up, still looking down and then wiped his eyes with the back of his hand.

They heard something coming from the room the sergeant identified as his son's room. "Let me, Sergeant. I'll check it out just in case." Opening the door, Captain Miller found the sergeant's son unharmed, crying on the floor.

The sergeant ran in and wrapped his son in an embrace, picking him up. Both were crying. "What happened here?" Sergeant Smith asked his son.

"Grandpa went to the store to get some food," his son began, tears streaming down his face as he recalled what happened. "He came back, and he had a bite on his arm. His arm was bleeding." The boy was crying too hard to go on.

"It's OK," the sergeant said, holding him until he was calm. "Keep going."

"Grandma told me to go to my room. She kept trying to call 9-1-1. But she couldn't get a signal I guess, And grandpa died." The tears poured once more, and he buried his face in his dad's chest.

"It's OK. You're safe now. Keep going."

The boy sniffled a few times and continued. "Then like an hour later, I heard Grandma screaming. I ran out there, and Grandpa was attacking her. I started screaming, and he came after me. I locked my door. He kept trying to get in." He sobbed. "I was so scared.

"I heard her scream again. Then I heard Clint at the door. He's our neighbor. And he was asking if everything was OK. I heard him open the door, and then he was screaming, and then chaos broke loose. I heard people yelling and screaming all over the place and some gunshots. I was really scared. I knew you would come for me. I just did." The tears turned to joy as he hugged his dad one more time.

"I would never leave you, son!" the sergeant said, pulling his son close. Then he spoke into the walkie. "Bradley, I have my son. Meet us in front in five."

"Lady, hey," Dickson said, trying to grab her arm.

"That's my boyfriend down the hall. See him?"

Dickson whispered into the walkie, "Captain, we got infected out here!

"Lady, that's not your boyfriend. Come back here. We got a situation here, sir! Lady! Get back. We need to leave now."

The woman screamed as the infected jumped on her.

Dickson fired at the infected.

Captain Miller burst out of 429. "Holy shit! Move fast now," he called as Dickson fired at more infected down the hall, killing more of the infected.

"Private Jackson, we're on our way out. Get ready. We have lots of infected behind us. Be ready."

"Yes, Captain!"

As Captain Miller and the others ran out into the street, Jackson yelled, "Get down!" Jackson starts to unload the fifty cal., taking down the infected behind them.

Hicks jumped up and yelled, "What the fuck are you doing?"

"I was saving your skin."

"You just let every infected in five miles know we're here, asshole," Hicks yelled back.

"He's right, Jackson. But thanks for your help. Hicks, Dickson, get in with Hayes. Sergeant, you and your son are with me."

"Bradley, where to now," Captain Miller asked?

"We need to reach the Acolyte facility."

"What is Acolyte?" Captain Miller asked.

"It's a research facility, the one I told you about. We need to get there as fast as possible," Bradley said.

"Sergeant, how far is this place from here?"

"About twenty minutes."

"Might as well be an hour in this shitstorm," Hicks said.

"What do you think, Captain?" the sergeant asked.

"It sounds like the best chance to get out of this hell. Let's do it."

"Listen. Keep on my ass, Bradley. And don't stop for shit. This could get bad. Got it?" the captain yelled over the radio.

As they looked out the windows, they saw people running, infected attacking people, buildings on fire, and people screaming for their help. And as they passed them, they felt helpless, for there was nothing they could do to help anyone.

"Private, keep your eyes on the road. Hicks, open on that fifty cal. Only fire if absolutely needed. Got it?" Captain Miller said.

"Yes, sir!"

As they traveled through more parts of downtown, they saw that people who were loitering and people who were hurting other people.

"Sergeant, this is bullshit. Why don't they bring in the army to help some of these people?"

"Captain, you know as well as I do this no longer about the people. It's about containing this outbreak," Bradley said.

"I know. It's just hard to watch and not able to help."

The city was far behind when the captain stopped them. "All right. We're stopping here. We're about a half a click from the building over that hill. From here, we go on foot," he said.

Bradley got out of the Hummer. "Why are we walking from here?"

"Because if there are a lot of infected, we need to be quiet, and"—the captain grabbed Bradley, shoving him against one of the Hummers—"we got you here. So you're going to tell me what's going on right now. What were you all doing in the town?"

"What town?" Bradley asked.

"Don't play with me. We lost men, civilians, not to mention all the shit we passed. What did you do there? I saw your package. I saw that same symbol on some of the equipment at the base. Now out with it," Captain Miller said.

"I was just sent in to get samples. That's it. The general was going to deliver this package himself, but he had an emergency in town. My wife is inside that facility, and she's sick. As far as I know, she's been infected. I need to get in there as well," Bradley pleaded with the captain.

"All right. Everyone, we're going to move to the facility. I don't know what's down there. So grab everything from the Hummers. We're going in quiet. Bradley, stay with me. I want Dickson and Hicks on point." The captain scanned all their faces. Some of them looked very grim and unsure of the reasons for this mission.

The sergeant saw this as well and spoke up. "Listen, I know you're all down from what we have seen out there, But the captain has never let me down, and he's not going to now. We need to find out how to stop this thing or at least warn the government so they can. So, let's go."

Everyone started to head out.

The sergeant went to grab his son out of the Hummer. Grabbing his jacket, the boy put it on. The sergeant kneeled to put his son's backpack on him and saw blood on his sleeve. "What's this?" the sergeant asked.

"Nothing. I just cut my arm getting into the car," Tom said.

"Want me to look at it?"

"No," Tom answered quickly. "I'm tough."

"That you are," the sergeant replied, rubbing his head. "Let's go."

The captain went over and fist-bumped the sergeant.

As they approached the facility, it looked gloomy in the evening haze, like something right out of a horror movie. Thick fog seemed to swallow the facility like a monster out of as swamp—as to say to them, "Enter if you dare."

Chapter 6

Compound V

"Dickson, you and Jackson go to the door and run a bypass. Jackson can do it according to his skill sets. Hicks and Hayes will keep you covered with sniper fire," the captain said.

"Yes, sir," everyone answered.

"The sergeant and his son will stay here for backup."

The sergeant replied, "Yes, sir."

The captain, Dickson, and Jackson wove their way toward the side door. The captain whispered, "Move out. Both of you keep your silencers on."

"I'm almost out of rounds for my silenced weapon, sir," Jackson replied.

"If you run out, do not switch to your Glock. You will bring more down on us, Private," the captain instructed.

"Yes, sir."

They approach the infected by the side door. Gunshots whispered through the air, and three infected went down. Dickson moved up to the door and looked around.

Dickson whistled and waved, signaling the all clear.

"Jackson, run a bypass."

"Yes sir, Captain." Jackson started the bypass on the door. "Fuck. This thing is fucking coded, sir. It's going to take just a little longer."

"Just go as fast as possible, Private. Our assess are on the line."

"Yes, sir. Almost there. One more minute."

Hicks looked through his scope and saw two infected come from around the corner. He aimed down his sights, and two shots whispered through the air, taking both infected down.

Captain Miller saw this and said into the walkie, "Nice shooting, Hicks."

"Don't worry, sir. We got your back. But you might want to hurry. There are a lot of them moving your way."

Captain Miller tapped Jackson on the shoulder. "Hurry it up, Private. We have more infected coming."

The captain and Dickson took aim as a group of infected came around the corner.

Hayes saw them through his sniper rifle. "I see them, sir. Taking them down now." He lines up his shot, and his gun clicked. "Fuck, Captain. I'm out. Hicks, you got a shot on my side?"

"I have no shot. Repeat, no shot," Hicks replied.

The captain and Dickson started taking down infected approaching on the right.

"Private, are you fucking in yet?" the captain yelled.

"Almost, sir. The last bit of security measures are giving me hell, sir." A moment later, Jackson yelled, "I got it, sir."

The door slid open.

The captain yelled into his radio, "It's now or never, Hicks. There a lot of infected moving toward us." He turned to his two privates. "Dickson, Jackson, get inside and secure the hall now. I'll hold them off till they get down here."

Dickson and Jackson moved inside to secure the entry and disappeared through the door.

The captain started shooting in small bursts of fire as everyone else started moving down the hill. The sergeant scooped up his son and started running down the hill behind the others. "Come on, Sergeant, or you and your son will be left out. So, move your ass," he yelled as they moved down the hill.

Hicks and Hayes got there from their sniper positions first. Hicks helped the captain take down infected.

Captain Miller, still providing cover, yelled, "Hayes, if your guns are out, get the fuck inside, or you will become a liability."

Hayes jumped inside the door. Bradley ran by Hicks and the captain, followed by the sergeant and his son.

"Captain, you go. I got this," Hicks said.

They were now shooting infected from both sides. The captain ducked inside, covering Hicks. "Move, Hicks, now."

Hicks made it inside, just before the infected swarmed the door. Hicks grabbed Jackson. "I thought you were good at hacking shit. You almost fucking killed us all."

Jackson yelled back, "Hey, man, that shit was military code. It took a lot longer than just a standard door." He pushed Hicks back.

"Bullshit," Hicks retorted.

Bradley said, "He's right. This facility is a military compound."

"What?" Hicks snapped. "You knew this the whole time. What the fuck do they do here? Bradley, what kind of facility is this? Is this where they made the so-called cure?"

"I know my wife works here. We worked together. She couldn't say what they were working on, but there were hints from her that it was called that." His eyes started to swelling up with tears. "She said she was sick. And if that means she's been infected, I don't know what I'll do." The tears streamed down his face.

Tom saw this and hugged him. "I'm sorry. I'm sure she will be OK," Tom said.

"Do you think your wife is infected?" the captain asked.

"I hope not," he said, drying his eyes and thanking Tom for the hug. "I think that's why they need this Compound V. I think it's the cure, but I don't know."

"Let's find this doctor and get some answers."

"My thoughts as well," Bradley said.

"Everyone move out and stay frosty. There could be infected in here," Captain Miller said.

The men reached the lab door.

Hicks peeked inside. "There are two women inside. They look like they're arguing."

Bradley came up beside Hicks and peered through the window. He recognized one of the doctors and knocked on the door.

"Who the hell is that? It's Brent! He's here to kill us." Monica was looking at the door where the sound came from and jumped back, frightened, his eyes widening.

"It's me, Rachael, Bradley. You asked me to bring Compound V, ma'am."

Rachael walked over and pushed the button, releasing the locks on the door.

Hicks, Jackson, and Dickson ran in. They were followed by Hayes and then Captain Miller and Bradley and, finally, the sergeant and his son Tom.

Rachael walked over and shook Bradley's hand. "Thank you for coming."

"Where's my wife?" Bradley said eagerly.

"She's in quarantine," Rachael replied, glancing over to Monica to make sure she didn't say anything. "Now please hand me the Compound V." She walked over to take it from Bradley.

"Not yet, ma'am. You need to tell us what's going on here. Then you'll get it," Captain Miller said, stepping in front of Bradley.

"Is she infected?" Bradley asked, looking past Captain Miller at Rachael.

"What?" Rachael answered, studying his face. "How do you know about the infection?" Rachael looked shocked, and again she turned to look at Monica, mumbling, "General Rhodes."

The captain quickly glanced over at Sergeant Smith, as if to say, Did you hear what she just said? Smith just shrugged his shoulders.

"How the hell do you know that name, ma'am?" the captain asked with confusion in his voice.

"He is a general who was dead set on trying out this compound for himself. He wouldn't listen to me. I'm afraid of what he is doing with it. How do you know that name, Captain?" Rachael asked back.

"He did exactly what you just said. Now the compound has infected thousands, if not more. We need to stop it or get ahold of someone who can help," Captain Miller said, watching for her reaction to this news.

"I told them this would happen, and they didn't listen." Rachael's eyes started to swell with tears. "It's all my fault. I created it." Tears streamed down her face.

"Please, Doctor, answer the question. Is she infected?" Bradley asked, sounding even more worried.

Rachael's face turned pale, and she stood silently for a moment, tears sliding down her cheeks. She turned away from him before she answered. "Yes."

Bradley fell to his knees. The sergeant grabbed his shoulder for comfort.

Wiping his eyes, Bradley asked, "With the compound I brought you, can you help her?"

"I don't know. We believe it might help prevent people from getting infected. But once you're infected, I'm just not sure," Rachael said, tears rolling down her face. In her mind, she thought of all those people who had died because of her. Wiping her eyes, she refocused. "I will do something to help everyone, even your wife if I can," she said and grabbed the briefcase from Bradley.

"Don't worry about that, Doctor. Please tell me what Compound Z is," Captain Miller asked.

"It was supposed to be a cure to the flu and common cold and pretty much anything, but the side effects where very severe."

"I think turning people into flesh-eating creatures is more than a side effect. Don't you agree, Doctor?" Hicks said.

"We also had an outbreak here," Rachael said.

"What do you mean? There was an outbreak in this facility?" Captain Miller said, looking very concerned. He glanced over at Sergeant Smith, and everyone seemed instantly more alert.

"It started in the morgue. A few of our test subjects died after being injected with Compound Z. They came back to life, attacking the doctors in the morgue."

"Didn't you contain it with the protocol you have in place here?" Bradley asked, jumping to his feet, his eyes widening.

"Of course, we did," Rachael replied. "We also sent in our security team. But they also died—all except one who broke out of the morgue and set them free. All those things are locked up in Lab B and the morgue."

Captain Miller questioned, "So how many people are still here alive?"

"There were four of us."

"Where are the other two?" Hayes asked, looking around the room only seeing the two women.

"Ed went to close off one of the corridors, and then he wanted to talk to Brent, the head security officer who broke out of the morgue," Rachael replied.

"Brent went crazy and grabbed Ed," Monica said, interrupting Rachael.

"So, where is Brent now?" Captain Miller asked.

"You guys have to get him back please," Monica said as she started crying.

"Right. All I care about is you trying to make a cure or whatever you need to do to stop this from spreading past Texas and into other parts of the United States," Captain Miller said.

"Captain, I can help Rachael and Monica to work on some kind of cure that also might save my wife," Bradley said, looking at both the women.

Bradley, Rachael, and Monica grabbed Compound V and started working.

"We're going to spread out and look for supplies and make sure this side of the facility is secure," the captain said.

"What do we do if we come across this Brent they were talking about, Captain?" Hayes asked.

"Do not engage unless engaged," the captain replied.

"*Yes, sir*!" everyone said.

"Hayes, I want you and Private Dickson to head out the door on the right and look for any supplies, medical, ammo anything. Hicks, Jackson, and I will take the bigger hallway on the left, Sergeant you stay here with the women and your son," Captain Miller said.

"Let me go with the Hayes and Dickson, sir."

"No, Sergeant. Your son needs you here. He's scared shitless. Besides, they know what they're doing."

"Yes, sir," the Sergeant replied, sounding disappointed.

"Move out, everyone. You know your job. We're not getting paid by the hour."

Hayes and Dickson moved through the hall down towards Lab B. Entering the lab, they saw a vial full of a bright green fluid and labeled, "Compound Z." Securing it, they moved into Lab C. Entering Lab C, they saw two infected people. Both were squirming in restraints and had blood running down their faces and mouths. The man wore a pilot's uniform, and the woman had black ooze running down her face.

"Captain, infected, tied down, one male and a female. Please advise what you'd like us to do with them? Over," Dickson said over his radio.

"Dickson, hold on. Do not engage."

"Rachael, why are there two infected in Lab C tied to tables?" The Sergeant asked, hearing the radio chatter.

"One is a pilot who was bitten, and the other is Bradley's wife," she replied.

Bradley stopped and looked at Rachael. "You tied her up like a fucking animal?" Tears streamed down his face again.

"We had to. She could have hurt herself or others. I'm sorry," Rachael said, hugging him. "Plus, we need them to try this new compound on. We need to see if it works."

"Dickson, leave them. We will deal with them later; we need some infected we can try the new compound on," the sergeant said, unable to keep the disgust from his voice. How could they treat these people like this?

"Roger that, sir," Dickson replied. "Moving into Lab A, sir. We will keep you posted."

"Thank you, Dickson. Over and out," the sergeant replied.

Hearing Dickson over the radio, Rachael grabbed the radio out of Sergeant Smith's hands. "Do not go in there," she cried.

Her warning came too late. Dickson and Hayes had just opened the door to Lab A, revealing subject 5. They saw that one of his arms was free. He had broken not just the straps but also his arm in different places. His arm was flailing as he tried to reach out toward Dickson and Hayes. His bones broken through the skin like little splinters. Black ooze ran down his arm, face, and mouth. Dickson felt his mouth fill with bile in the back of his throat looking at this. Subject 5's skin was pale, and patches of it looked like raw chicken set out to rot.

Hayes got on the radio, eyeing Dickson, who looked like he was going to lose his lunch. "We have an infected with black ooze coming out of it. Should we put this one down?"

"Why is one of these infected with black ooze in your lab?" Sergeant Smith said angrily.

"Subject 5 is the result of a different compound, called X. We can still use him to see if Compound V will work on him as well," Rachael replied.

"Dickson, Hayes, lock that lab up tight. Then meet us after you finish your sweep. We will deal with him later."

Meanwhile, the captain, Hicks, and Jackson made sure the other hallway was secure. They had just headed down to the security office when they started to hear voices down the hall.

The captain gestured to Jackson to take a position by the door. From there, they listened to a man they surmised was Brent.

The captain whispered on his radio, "I believe we have found Brent and Ed."

"What's going on with them, Captain?"

"Brent has another guy—I'm assuming Ed—tied to a chair with a grenade taped around his mouth and is asking him crazy questions," Jackson reported after peeking into the room. "What would you want us to do?"

"Please stand by, Captain. Let me advise Rachael. Hold tight," the sergeant said.

"Rachael, Captain Miller and his men have found Brent in the security office. Is there any reason we need him alive?"

"No, none I can think of. Why do you ask?"

"Because they found him with Ed."

"Is Ed all right?" Monica asked, looking very worried.

"For the moment, yes. But Brent has him tied to a chair with a grenade taped to his mouth. We can try to save Ed by taking out Brent, but there is a chance Ed will die."

"I see. The only thing is Brent has the main security card that can open up any door in the facility," Rachael replied.

"How important is this card, Doctor?"

"Without it, we can't open all doors from this room. Instead, they'll have to be opened manually with my code, which means someone might have to stay behind if we need to escape."

"Thank you, Doctor, for your information," the sergeant said before relaying the information to the captain.

"What are you going to do?" he asked.

"I'm going to kill Brent and get that card if we can."

"What about Ed, sir?" Jackson asked still looking into the room.

"Save him, if possible. But we need that security card," Captain Miller said.

The captain crouched over by the open door next to Jackson and Hicks. "Hicks, Jackson, follow my lead. Do not fire until I do. Understand?"

Both answered, "yes, sir."

The captain, Hicks, and Jackson crept through the open door, now able to hear Brent talk more clearly.

"So, Ed, have you changed your mind? You want to come with me and gut those two bitches? I can't hear you. Cat got your tongue? Or is it just a grenade?" Brent started laughing.

Tears flowed down Ed's face on hearing Brent make stupid jokes about him. Looking down to see the duct tape holding his arms and legs in place, Ed felt something attached to his mouth. For a spilt second, Ed saw someone peek into the room. At first, he hoped it was an infected. Then he thought twice. He didn't want to become one of them. Seeing movement again, he now knew he had seen someone. Just then, someone came into the room crouching. Ed's eyes widened.

Seeing the reaction, Brent grabbed his AR-15 and got behind Ed.

"Come on, who's fucking out there? Answer me or this motherfucker gets it. You think I'm playing?" Brent's gun was on Ed's shoulder, pointing at the door, and his other hand was on the detonator.

"I'm Captain Miller with Special Forces. Brent, put down your weapons, and you will not be harmed."

Brent's face turned red with anger. "I won't be harmed you say," he shouted. "Those bitches already tried killing me. I need to return the favor."

"Don't be stupid. You're outmanned and outgunned. They are not worth it."

"I know what those cunts did. I know all about the infection they released. It's only a matter of time, and we're all dead already. So why should I?"

"Captain, we don't have time for this. Let's put a fucking bullet in his brain and call it a day," Hicks said, peeking over the counter.

Hicks stood up from behind the tool counter. "Listen, dipshit. We don't have time for this, so lower your weapon, or you die. Got it?"

Captain Miller stood up. His gun was also trained on Brent. "Brent, just hand over the security card and drop your weapon please. We don't want to kill you."

Brent showed his other hand, which had a detonator in it. "I press this, and we all die."

Hicks fired a shot, hitting him in the arm and making him drop it.

Brent shrieked in pain. "You motherfuckers." He started firing his AR-15 right at Hicks and the captain, and they ducked behind the counter and returned fire, missing Brent.

Hicks took a bullet in the arm that knocked him back against the wall. He fell to the floor, clutching his arm. Looking down at his arm, he saw it was just a graze with a little blood coming out of it.

Captain Miller continued firing at Brent as Brent jumped through another door to the side of him.

As Brent dived, he grabbed the detonator with his hand. He yelled from behind the door, "Fuck you, motherfuckers," and pushed the detonator.

"Get down," the captain yelled and jumped on top of Jackson.

The grenade in Ed's mouth went off, exploding his head and body into pieces. Blood splattered on every wall in the room, and bones and flesh were hanging everywhere.

"Are you all right, Jackson?"

"Yeah, I'm fine. How's Hicks?"

The captain leaned over to Hicks. "You all right, Hicks?"

Hicks coughed and gave Captain Miller a thumbs-up.

The captain's radio came to life with the sergeant on the other end. "Captain, did we just hear an explosion?"

"Some sort of charge went off set off by Brent."

"Any casualties?"

"Yeah, Ed. I believe Brent escaped."

"What about the security card, Captain?"

"Brent had it around his neck."

"Meet back at the lab, Captain. Rachael wants to talk to you."

"We are on our way. Over and out," Captain Miller said.

Looking down at his wound, Brent saw black ooze, not blood. His head was killing him and spinning. He started to black out, thinking as he did, *Got some more people to kill.*

Chapter 7

The Cure

Seeing Captain Miller come back, Rachael asked him to come over. As he did, she handed him an iPad. He looked down at it. Not really sure what he was looking at, he handed it back.

"We're done," she explained. "We took cells from Compound V and Compound Z. It attacks the infected cells, killing any infection from Compound Z. So, if they are bitten by someone who is infected, it will automatically attack the cells of the infection. It should inoculate everyone."

Captain Miller was watching the iPad as Rachael brought up her notes. "What about someone who's already infected?"

"We're not sure. We're going to need to test it," Rachael said, looking at Bradley with a frown and wishing she knew.

Bradley looked over to Rachael. "Will it help my wife?"

"I don't know. She died and came back," Rachael said, her eyes not meeting his.

Hayes and Dickson come into the room.

"Sir, we didn't find anything. Just some medical supplies and a door locked down the corridor. We also found another door that leads to the outside to a helicopter pad."

"Were there any infected, Hayes?"

"Yes, sir. A few we could see outside the door."

"Thank you, Hayes."

"Captain Miller, I need to talk to you outside please," Dickson said, glancing over to Rachael.

"Sir, Bradley's wife is one of those infected with the black ooze coming out of her, but she's different. She's not as aggressive as we've seen, but she's definitely one of them. And subject 5 must be one of the first. He looks bad, like he's been in there for a while." Dickson's face went pale as he remembered what he'd seen.

"Rachael, please come out here," Captain Miller called from the hall.

Rachael walked out into the hall, and Captain Miller looked her straight in the eye. "Why didn't you tell us that Bradley's wife was one of the other infected? She has black ooze running down her face. Those we've seen before like that are incredibly aggressive, their bites turn others quicker, and they don't die like the others."

"Nancy came up with Compound X herself. I helped her along where I could. She believed so deeply it was the cure she gave herself a small dose. She got sick and then died. If Compound V works, we can help everyone," Rachael said, staring right back at Captain Miller.

As they walked back in everyone looked at them. Rachael was the first to speak. "Are we ready to try Compound V?"

Monica change the subject. "Wait a minute. None of you found Ed?" There was panic in her voice.

Captain Miller looked at Monica but couldn't meet her eyes. "Sorry, ma'am. Ed was killed by Brent."

"What?" Monica shrieked. "You didn't bring his body back with the equipment. We might have saved him."

Captain Miller glanced over to Hicks and then back to Monica. "Ma'am, you don't understand."

"I understand too well, Captain. Because he is not one of your soldiers, he just gets left behind." Monica's face filled with anger and tears rolled down her face.

"Listen, you crazy bitch, his head was blown off his fucking body. If you want, here's a bag. Go ahead and start scooping," Hicks shouted back.

"Jesus, Hicks." Jackson was surprised by Hicks's tone. He watched Monica run out of the room crying.

"Well, she is blaming us, like we just left him. Someone had to tell her."

Rachael, sounding annoyed, picked up where they'd left off. "All we can do is inject her and see what happens. That's all I can offer."

Bradley shook his head and brought his hands to his head, holding back tears. Thinking of his wife, he wished he could just hug her one more time.

Everyone walked out the door to go to lab C, where Bradley's wife was held. As Bradley walked into the room, he saw Nancy. It was all he could do to keep himself from going to her and hugging her. Seeing her like this was breaking his heart. Bradley looked at Rachael. "What do we need to do?"

Rachael loaded the vial into the syringe gun. The liquid was bright blue and glowing, looking like it had real power. Rachael stared at it, hoping it would work. "Please hold her as still as possible while I inject her."

Bradley and the Captain grabbed Nancy by her arms, and Hicks held her head down with a belt to keep her from biting anyone.

Rachael injected her with the cure.

Then they held down the pilot, injecting him as well. A minute after the pilot was injected, his body started convulsing, and his eyes started to bleed blue liquid. His eyes went wide and then exploded out of their sockets, like light bulbs bursting from a light socket. His body went limp, and he fell still, dead once again—this time for good.

Everyone looked over to Nancy, who also started to shake. Bright red neon blood, no longer black ooze, started to flow from her eyes. For a second, her heart beat, and then it stopped. Nancy's body lay still once again. Bradley cried out and leaned over her body, giving her a last hug. Everyone looked grim. Bradley tried to grab Rachael, and Captain Miller grabbed him before he could.

"This is your fault," Bradley yelled at her through his sobs. "You're going to go to hell for this."

"I said I might be able to help her, even before the injection," Rachael said with fear in her voice.

Monica burst into the door.

"Sergeant, you need to come quickly. Your son fainted."

Everyone left the room and went to check on the sergeant's son—everyone except for Bradley.

Rachael leaned down to examine Tom.

"What's wrong with him?" asked Sergeant Smith. His voice sounded hoarse as he bent over to grab Tom's hand.

"He's infected."

"What?" Hicks asked.

Rachael looked at his arm. Seeing blood, she pulled back his shirt. "He has a scratch on his arm."

"I thought you checked him, Sergeant."

"Captain, I'm sorry. I was going to, but I forgot when we got jumped by infected in the apartment building."

"Rachael, can you give him the antidote? He hasn't died." Sergeant Smith asked, his voice heavy with concern.

"I don't know if it will even work," Rachael said worriedly.

"He's either going to die by the infection or by the injection. I'd rather it be the injection so I don't have to put my own son down," the sergeant said.

"Fine. Monica, load up one more injection."

"Yes, ma'am."

Monica drew another injection. "Here you go, Rachael," she said, handing over the vial.

Holding the syringe, Rachael lowered it toward Tom's arm. Her hand started to shake. Sergeant Smith held his son in one arm. He took his other hand and put it one top on Rachael's shaking hand to steady it. He looked her right in the eyes. "Everything will be all right," he said.

Looking into his eyes, Rachael could see he was trying to hold back tears. She injected the antidote into Tom's arm.

In just a few minutes, Tom's skin started to look better, and he woke up.

"Dad, what's going on?" Tom asked.

"Why didn't you tell me you were scratched?" Sergeant Smith said, hugging him and feeling the joy of his son hugging him back.

"I was afraid you would be mad. I'm sorry," Tom said, tears falling down his face.

Rachael grabbed Tom's arm and took his pulse. "How do you feel, Tom?"

"I feel better. My headache is gone, and my stomach doesn't hurt anymore."

"I would like to get a blood sample if that's all right?" Rachael looked to Sergeant Smith.

"Go ahead, Doc," the sergeant replied.

Rachael took a blood sample and went over to her lab to examine the sample.

"I can't believe it. It worked. The infection is gone. We need to give everyone the antidote now."

Bradley walked into the room. "Sorry about earlier. I know you didn't mean to kill her. She's just all I had," Bradley said, his voice still hoarse.

"I know, Bradley. I'm sorry for your loss. Nancy was a huge part of our team. I wish …" Rachael trailed off, not knowing how to say she was missing Nancy not just as a friend but also as a researcher.

"What is it, Rachael?" Bradley asked.

"She was working on how we could release Compound Z into the air and inoculate everyone at once. I bet if we use her research, we could do the same thing with Compound V. It will kill the infected and inoculate everyone at the same time."

"Wait. You're saying we can turn this into a weapon and an antidote at the same time?" the captain asked.

"Yes. You saw what it did to Nancy. We can test it on the infected locked in the morgue section—pump the hallways with the gas and see what happens."

"Do we even have enough of it to test it?" Monica asked.

"We should have just enough after I give us all the injection first."

Rachael and Monica gave everyone, including themselves, an injection.

"There. We have enough for just one try. After we pump the gas, we wait for about twenty minutes. Then we'll have to go in and check for ourselves. All the cameras in the hallways are not working. The only one still functioning is the camera by the main door, and the only one who had access to it was Brent and his security staff."

"Wait. You said only security can access the main door; how do we get out of this place then?" Captain Miller asked.

"That's just for the main access door. We can override any other door at our console here. The only problem is someone has to stay at the console to both open and close them," Monica replied.

"That might be a problem," Jackson said.

"We will deal with it when that time comes, Private," Captain Miller said.

"Yes, sir," Jackson replied.

"We're all set up," Dickson said.

"Dickson and I set everything just as the doctor ordered. We're ready to start to pump the gas on your ready, sir," Hayes reported.

"Proceed, Hayes," the captain said.

They started pumping the gas into the ducts that led into the morgue and surrounding hallways.

Some of the gas leaked into the security office. The fumes woke Brent up. He looked down at the bullet wound in his arm. It bled black ooze, not blood. He smiled as he saw that his wound was close to healed and thought to himself, *Those motherfuckers are trying to kill me with gas. I'll kill them all.*

Dickson looks at the gauges. "That's it, ma'am. All canisters are empty."

"Thank you, Dickson. Hopefully, this works," Rachael said.

"I guess we sit and wait. Does anyone have a deck of cards?" Hicks asked.

"Dickson, how long has it been?" Captain Miller asked when they all had waited as long as they thought they could stand.

"Twenty, sir," Dickson replied.

"Jackson, Dickson, and Hayes will enter the morgue area. Hicks and I will stay at the door for cover just in case the infected are not dead. Sergeant, you will stay here with Bradley and the doctors," Captain Miller said.

"Yes, sir," everyone replied.

Jackson, Dickson, and Hayes approached the hallway door. "Dr. Morgan, the doors are locked down," Hayes said.

"OK, once I open the door from here, it will close again. I can't hold it open without the main security card." Rachael opened the door with the press of a button. After hitting the button, she called for Monica to come to her and whispered to her, “I want you to get me samples of Nancy’s blood. I need to analyze it.”

Monica looked confused but did as she was asked.

“Hicks and I will take positions outside the hall door to cover you if you need to get out of there in a hurry,” Captain Miller said.

Hayes, Jackson, and Dickson made their way down the hall, the mist in the air making it hard for them to see.

“Captain, we have dead bodies here, down the hall, about four or five,” Hayes said.

“Do they look like they were infected, Hayes?”

“Can’t tell, sir. They’re all missing their heads. Looks like what happened to Nancy. Over,” Hayes replied.

“Hold your position, Hayes,” the captain said. “Rachael, do you copy?”

“Yes, Captain, I’m here. Go ahead.”

“The team found bodies with heads that are missing. Looks like the results of Compound V. Over.”

“I have given Jackson some supplies to get samples for me. Please have him do so and then have them proceed to the morgue,” Rachael replied.

“Yes, ma’am. Captain over and out. Jackson, did you hear the doc?”

“Yes, sir. Getting samples as we speak. I will let you know when we reach the morgue, sir.”

“Thank you, Jackson. Over and out,” Captain Miller said.

Approaching the door, the men saw debris everywhere. It looked like someone had blown the door wide open. Hayes held up his hand to stop Jackson and Dickson. He peeked in and saw bodies everywhere. It looked as if they had all been infected. But it also looked like the aftermath of a bloodbath, with half eaten corpses and body parts that had clearly been ripped off strewn about the room. He waved for Jackson and Dickson to move up. The three entered the morgue, and Hayes pointed for the two of them to move into the other room.

Grabbing the radio, he reported, “Looks like the door’s been blown open. But there are just bodies in here—all infected, all dead.”

As they swept through the first adjoining room, Jackson and Dickson could see the torn limbs of the people who used to work in this area and security personnel, bodies that looked like hamburgers half eaten by the infected.

"Listen up, both of you. We are not here to do an investigation. We're here to make sure all these fucking infected are dead. Dr. Morgan followed proper protocol and locked down the area."

"At least we know that Compound V works on these things," Dickson said.

"It's been a long time, sir. Should we go in and make sure they're OK?" Hicks said.

Just then, the captain's radio crackled to life.

"Captain, do you read me? The sweep is clear. All infected are dead. Over."

After meeting up with the captain and Hicks, the stunned trio headed back to the main lab, not knowing what was waiting just behind the corner in the dark.

Brent waited for the five military men to pass before heading down toward the main door. He paused to look at his arms, feeling whatever it was that was flowing through his veins, as black as the night, move through his body like worms. He saw that the bullet hole had now closed; only a black mark with the black ooze pouring out remained. Feeling better than he had in a long time, Brent felt the anger rising in him. *I will kill them all.* He laughed to himself. *I will open the main door and watch them all squirm.*

The captain and squad entered the lab.

Jackson saw Rachael. "Here you go, Doc. The samples you asked for. What did you need them for?"

"Thank you, Jackson. I want to see how the gas reacted to the infection. And I want to determine if we might need to up the power of the gas for a bigger crowd," Rachael replied.

"The only place we can get our hands on enough Compound V is the Eagle's Nest facility," Monica said.

Rachael's thoughts went to Jessica. Eagle's Nest was her research facility. Would she help them? And if she did, would she try to take control of the cure for herself? She knew how Jessica was.

Hayes remembered something he'd noticed on their way in. "There is a helicopter out the back door. We might have to fight our way there, but that would be the fastest way to get to this other facility."

"I think that would be the best option right now. Everyone get your gear. We move out in five minutes," Captain Miller said.

"Hey, Captain?" Dickson said.

"What is it, Private?" Captain Miller replied.

"Who the hell is that at the front gate?" Dickson said, looking at one of the monitors.

Hicks joined him at the monitor. "Holy shit. That's fucking Brent."

"What the fuck is he doing?"

"He is going to open the door with the security key. He is going to let the infected in," Rachael said, looking up.

Captain Miller shouted, "We need to move now!"

"First of all, someone needs to stay here to open the door from the panel because of the security lockdown system," Rachael said. "That's why we needed Brent's key. Second, we don't even know how big the chopper out there is. As far as we know, it may only have two seats."

"I don't think we have any other options. We need to get out there and see what's out there. We will figure it out when we get there," Captain Miller said.

Rachael looked around. "Who will stay here and open the door?"

"I'll stay," Monica said.

"What?" Rachael replied, stunned.

Monica looked grim but answered, "I know how to operate the panel."

"Captain, take the men and get to the chopper. I will stay with Monica and hold off the infected so she can activate the panel. I'll just need a gun,

Captain," Bradley said, feeling confident. He grabbed Monica's hand to comfort her.

"You sure about this?" Captain Miller asked, handing Bradley a weapon.

"Yes. My wife is gone. I think this is what she would want me to do, Captain. Now go," Bradley said.

Dickson watched on the monitor as Brent approached the giant main doors of the facility, slid his key into the slot on the panel next to the doors, and pressed a series of buttons. The doors slid open, alarms started to wail, and he looked at the camera right by the door and flipped it off before walking back down the hall.

"*We need to move*!" Dickson yelled.

Everyone but Dr. Bradley and Monica prepared to leave for the back helicopter pad.

"Look," Monica said, calling Rachael back to the camera. Together, they watched Brent walking down the hall, the infected running past him as if he wasn't even there. "How is that possible?" Monica asked, stunned.

"I don't know," Rachael replied, but she did think back to those first injections she had given Brent and his brother.

The captain grabbed Rachael by her arm, interrupting her thoughts. "We have got to go!"

They reached the back door, and the captain grabbed his radio. "Monica, we are at the back door. Please open. Over."

"Yes, Captain. It will be open in a minute."

The captain looked at everyone. "Listen up. Hicks, you're on point when the door opens. Dickson, my right. Jackson, my left. Hayes and I will bring up the rear. Sergeant, you, Tom, and Rachael stay in the middle. The sergeant and the doc are the main priority."

"Man, don't we all need to get to the chopper, Captain?" Hicks said.

"Hey, dipshit. Can you fly a helicopter?" Hayes asked.

"No," Hicks replied.

"Can you mix up a cure to save everyone?" Hayes asked, looking annoyed.

"*No*," Hicks said sourly.

"Then they get on the chopper first, just like the captain said," Hayes snapped.

The back door slid open, and everyone filed outside.

"Move," yelled the captain.

They formed up just as the captain said.

"Infected on the right," Dickson yelled.

They all stopped as a unit. Shots from their rifles took down the infected. The squad moved out again.

"Fuck! We have infected by the chopper," Hicks yelled.

Once again, they all stopped as one unit and fired at the infected, taking them down with just a few shots.

They finally reached the chopper.

Hicks got to the chopper. "Oh, this is fucking great. It only has four seats."

Hayes turns to Captain Miller. "So, who's going with the doctor, sir?"

"Hicks, shut the fuck up. Jackson and the sergeant and his son will go," Captain Miller instructed. "Tom will be a liability here, and Jackson knows about piloting. The sergeant will need a copilot."

Hayes and the captain started to help Rachael and the sergeant's son into the chopper. "Here, Captain. You'll need this if you're going to meet us at the Eagle's Nest." Rachael handed him her ID card.

"Thank you, Dr. Morgan," Captain Miller said.

"My name is Rachael, and Godspeed, Captain," Rachael said.

"Oh, this is bullshit," Hicks complained.

The captain grabbed Hicks. "Listen. I'm tired of your mouth and your bullshit, Hicks. You need to shut the fuck up and fall in. You're a fucking solider. Now act like it. Get your gear. We need to go help Bradley and Monica. Got it?" Captain Miller said.

As the captain and Hicks were arguing, Dickson and Hayes were taking down some more infected coming at them. "I don't mean to break up this romance, sir, but there are a lot of incoming infected," Hayes said, shooting.

The chopper took off, and the sergeant looked down and gave a thumbs-up as they left the area, on their way to the Eagle's Nest.

"Move out. We need to double-time back to the lab. I just hope we're not too late."

Hayes looked at Captain Miller. "Too late for what, sir?"

"To help Bradley and Monica. Now move like you got a purpose." Captain Miller ran for the door.

His three remaining men followed close, all four firing and taking down infected on their way back into the facility.

"The back door is open. The captain has exited the facility," Monica said.

"Good, because we're about to have company. There are about twenty infected coming up the tunnel," Bradley said.

Just then, the infected arrived, slamming their bodies against the lab door again and again. Before long, the door started to break.

Bradley heard the scream of the infected grow louder. "Monica, get behind me now. The door won't hold much longer."

"What will you do if there are too many?" Monica asked, panic starting to sound in her voice.

"I'll kill us both. We're not going out like that," Bradley said, holding the gun tight and aiming at the door.

At that moment, the first infected broke through the crack in the door, and Bradley took it down right away.

"Nice shot," Monica said.

Another infected came through, and Bradley fired again. The door started to give more. This time, two infected burst in at once, and Bradley quickly took them down.

"How many shots do have you left in the gun?" Monica shrieked.

"I have about fifteen in this clip," Bradley said, looking a little worried.

Three infected burst into the room, and Bradley took them down, though the third got awfully close to Bradley.

"Holy crap, that was close."

"If there any more than three, we might have a problem," Bradley said.

Just then, what remained of the door smashed to the ground, and ten infected piled into the room, heading straight at them.

"Get down!" a voice behind them yelled.

Bradley grabbed Monica and pulled her to the floor. Just as they hit the floor, shots rang and bullets flew, taking down all the infected that had come through the door.

Bradley got up off the floor and saw the captain, Hicks, Hayes, and Dickson standing there with their guns smoking. "Captain, what the hell are you doing here?"

"Chopper only had four seats. We need to get back to the Hummers and meet the others at Eagle's Nest. We need to hurry. There will be more infected coming."

"Someone still needs to stay back and open the side door where we came in," Dickson said.

"I'll do it," Monica replied.

"Monica, whoever stays is going to die," Captain Miller said.

"I'm a liability. At least this way I can help you guys. Besides, I'm the only one who knows how to work the panel," Monica replied.

"I'm staying with her," Bradley said.

"I can't ask you to do that," Monica said, tears in her eyes.

"She's right. If you do this, you will die," Captain Miller said.

"There nothing left for me out there. At least here, I can help. There's no time to argue. Leave before more show up. Now," Bradley said.

All four men ran for the side door through which they'd first entered the facility.

Monica opened the door. "Captain, the door's open."

"Thank you, Monica," the captain said as the men slipped out the side door and ran toward the waiting vehicles.

Monica released the button, closing the side door. Bradley grabbed the rifle and got ready, as they could hear infected running down the hall. Firing, he took down all five and then turned to her. "Maybe we can find another room and lock it down to give us a better chance."

Just as he said that, his head exploded, leaving Monica's face covered in blood and brains. Monica screamed.

She heard a voice coming from down the hall. "Nice makeup, bitch. It looks the same as your boyfriend Ed's brains." Brent started laughing.

Chapter 8

Eagle's Nest

Jessica Price was very strong-willed, attractive, and power hungry. Her power had really started growing with her husband's success as a politician. She'd been on many projects and had taken the lead at many labs. When her husband became vice president, she got to be head of the secret military facility known as Eagle's Nest. The facility was run by General Rhodes, who was very close to the vice president. Jessica used her new power to take credit for many of her scientists' work. It was there that she had learned about a young scientist who was working on a compound that could not only wipe out widespread ailments like the common cold but also make advances in extending life if successful. She used her power to become the lead and oversee the young scientist at the Acolyte facility, where she can watch her closely.

As Sergeant Smith flew the chopper over some houses, he directed Jackson's attention to the gruesome scene below them. The infected were swarming people's houses and apartments, attacking and killing anything in their path with no warning. They saw civilians running from their homes, trying to wave down the helicopter. Civilians on top of apartments jumped to their deaths, instead of being attacked by the infected.

Some people tried to stand their ground, attacking or firing their weapons but having little effect on the horde swallowing their homes and loved ones.

"Sir, we need to do something. Can't we get the ahold of the government to help? They have contingency plans for this, right?!" Jackson felt anger swelling inside him at the sight of all this.

"Jackson, there is nothing we can do, with all communications not just down but seemingly blocked somehow. If we go down there, those people will swarm the chopper. The best thing we can do for these people is get the doc to the lab so she can make that cure. Maybe at the lab we can contact the government," Sergeant Smith said, also feeling sad and angry.

"By the time she makes it, these people will be dead, sir," Jackson said, looking down at the chaos—the fires breaking out, the people trying to wave down the chopper.

One car plowed through people to get away, and those who could jumped on top of it, as if hoping it could be their escape too.

"I know it sucks. But the faster we get there, the more we will save," the sergeant replied. "Dr. Morgan, I see the facility. We will arrive in five minutes."

"Thank you, Sergeant," Rachael replied.

A security guard walked into Jessica's office.

"What is it? I told you I didn't want to be disturbed," Price said, face full of rage.

"Sorry, ma'am. But there is a helicopter coming," the security guard said sheepishly.

"Is it my husband?" Price asked.

"No, ma'am. It has the markings of Acolyte facility," he replied.

Price looked up at the security officer. "Get Marissa. I want her to greet them. Bring them straight to my office," Price said, looking back at her papers.

"Yes, ma'am," he replied and walked out of her office.

The sergeant set down the chopper and stepped out. He was greeted by a woman named Marissa, who introduced herself as the head security officer and extended her hand.

"You must be the welcome wagon," the sergeant said, shaking her hand.

"You all need to come with me. Jessica Price is waiting for you in her office," Marissa said, turning and walking down the ramp toward the entrance.

Rachael and Sergeant Smith glanced at each other and started to follow her down the ramp, the others following them. As Rachael approached, Marissa said, "Nice to see you again, ma'am," holding the door open.

Marissa opened the door to Price's office. "Ma'am, there here," she announced as they walked in.

Rachael had been waiting a long time to tell Jessica Price off. Now she would get the chance to nail her ass to the wall for letting this happen. She could see her face now. She grinned as she imagined it, walking through the door into Price's office.

At first, Jessica didn't look up from her computer, finally looking up at the door with a surprised look on her face.

"What the hell are you doing here?" Jessica asked, frowning.

"I'm here to fix your huge fuckup," Rachael said, smiling.

"What are you talking about?" Jessica replied.

"I'm talking about the horde of infected heading this way," Rachael said.

"We're working on a solution as we speak," Jessica said.

"While you've been working on one, I have one. And I'm going to help you, so this doesn't get worse, and then you're going to resign as head researcher," Rachael said with a blank face.

"Really, just like that? You say you have a solution. May I ask what you think you have? Jessica said.

"I not only have a cure to Compound Z, I also have a weapon against the infected that will kill them," Rachael said.

"What did you come here for? To rub it in my face?"

"No. What I need is Compound V. Seeing you squirm is a bonus," Rachael replied.

"Compound V? You said it yourself. It doesn't work," Jessica said.

"I don't have time to explain right now. Please let me work on this, and then I will tell you everything once we have the infection dealt with," Rachael said.

Jessica stared at Rachael for a minute before hitting an intercom button on her desk.

"Ellen, will you please come into my office," Jessica said into the intercom.

"Yes, ma'am, on my way," Ellen replied.

Ellen walked through a back door into Jessica's office.

"Hello, ma'am. What can I do for you?" Ellen asked.

"Ellen, this is Rachael Morgan, head researcher at Acolyte. And this is Ellen, my top researcher here," Jessica said.

Rachael and Ellen shook hands.

"Ellen, please show Dr. Morgan to the lab where we keep Compound V," Jessica said.

"What? Compound V?" Ellen asked, surprised.

"Yes, Compound V. She thinks she can use it as an antidote for Compound Z," Jessica said.

"We already tried, but it didn't work," Ellen said.

"Just do it now, Ellen," Jessica said angrily.

"Yes, ma'am," Ellen said with a little fear in her voice. "Please follow me," Ellen said to Rachael.

"We're also waiting for some more men to arrive. They may be coming in hot with the infected," the sergeant said, interrupting them.

"Marissa, please have your men prepare for their arrival. And show these men where they can wait," Jessica said.

"Yes, ma'am," Marissa said, waving for her men to follow, along with Jackson and Sergeant Smith and his son.

"Thank you," Rachael replied.

Ellen led Rachael out the back door to the labs.

As soon as everyone was gone, Jessica picked up the phone and dialed.

"Get me the president!" she said into the phone and then a moment later, "Sir, we have a solution to fight the infected and a possible cure."

"I will send the general and the vice president," the president said.

Jessica hung up the phone and walked out to the front office to see a sergeant standing outside the door.

"Is there something I can help you with?" Price asked.

"Where did Ellen take Dr. Morgan?" the sergeant asked, looking her straight in the eyes.

"She said she could help with what's going on, and my head scientist took her back to the lab to work on a cure, as she called it. So if you don't mind lowering your weapons, we're on the same side, whatever your name is," Jessica said with rudeness in her voice.

"I want to see the doctor; I don't know you to just to take your word. I am here to protect her, and you can call me Sergeant," Sergeant Smith said.

"I'll take you to the lab so you can see for yourself, Sergeant," she said.

"After you, ma'am," Sergeant Smith said.

Jessica and Sergeant Smith walked down the hall, going through a door marked, "Labs." As they approach the labs, Sergeant Smith saw people working.

"What the hell do you do here?" Sergeant Smith asked.

"That's classified," Rebecca replied.

"Classified as in making a fucking poison to turn everyone onto fucking infected killing machines?" Sergeant Smith said in a serious voice.

"Sergeant, we have to protect against every possible scenario that anyone can throw at us, and sometimes our projects don't turn out," she replied angrily.

"What happens when they go bad like this? Are you trying to cover up your role in this tragic situation?" the sergeant retorted angrily.

"Sometimes we do things that are for the best interest of the people whether they know it or not. If we told everyone right now there was an infection killing people, how do you think the nation would act? It could break down into chaos. We clean it up like nothing happened so the people can go on with their lives. It's the same with you, Sergeant. You follow orders because you know it's for the greater good."

They both walked down the hall to the next set of labs, and the sergeant saw Rachael working with another scientist.

Sergeant Smith looked at Jessica. "Open the door."

"If you want to talk to her, use the intercom," Jessica said.

Sergeant Smith pressed the intercom button. "Rachael, are you all right?"

"Yes. Why? Is there a problem?" she asked.

"No problem. Just wanted to make sure you are OK."

"Thank you, Sergeant. I am fine. In fact, Ellen and I have almost completed the formula and will soon be ready to put it into the computer for processing."

"I will be in my office. Please come and find me when the formula is ready. I would like to see you before that happens," Jessica said.

"I will see you in a few," Rachael replied.

"Please make yourself at home while we wait for Rachael to finish the formula. I will be in my office," Jessica said and walked back to her office.

The sergeant walked into the room where his son and Jackson were waiting.

Jackson saw Sergeant Smith. "So, what do we now?"

"Let's go get some food and then see if their radio is up so we can try to contact the captain," Sergeant Smith replied.

Rachael and Ellen entered Jessica's office with a data card in Ellen's hand.

"Jessica, the formula is ready. Please give me the key to the processing machine so I can input the formula and start mixing it," Rachael said.

"Let me have the formula please," Jessica said, extending her hand to take it from Ellen.

"Why?" Rachael asked suspiciously.

"Because I want to see this miracle formula for myself," Jessica replied.

"We don't have time for this," Rachael pleaded.

"Now, Ellen," Jessica snapped.

"Don't do it, Ellen. She's hiding something. Tell me why you want it now, Jessica," Rachael demanded.

"We all can be very rich with an antidote to this thing. Just think of the millions of people who will pay for this—the countries that will pay for this. We have a gold mine here," Jessica explained.

"What? You want this for money? What about the thousands who will die if we don't get this out there to kill the infected first?" Rachael's face reddened with anger.

Jessica laughed. "We let it spread a little more, and then we say we found a cure, and millions will pay after they see what happened. Everyone will want to protect their families. And on top of that, we will get all the funding we will ever need." She pressed the button for her intercom. "Marissa, please come in here.

Marissa walked into the office. "Yes, ma'am."

"Please grab the security card and bring it to me," Jessica said.

Now Rachael laughed. "Go ahead. Kill us. Without us, you can't make any more. You don't know the right order of the compound."

Marissa stopped. She had seen this too many times—Jessica ordering her to take something or steal something so Jessica could come out on top. And the careers of those people were ruined, tossed to the wayside while Jessica got more and more power. She was done. Not again. Too many lives were at stake.

"Marissa, did you hear me?" Jessica snapped angrily.

Marissa turned to look at Jessica and pulled her sidearm, pointing it right at her. "No, ma'am, not this time."

Jessica's face dropped from a smile to a frown. "What the hell are you doing?"

"Too many times I've watched you ruin someone's life. Not this time. I'm stopping you right now," Marissa said, pushing her into her chair.

Just then, Sergeant Smith and Jackson walked into Jessica's office.

"What the hell is going on?" the sergeant asked.

Rachael looked at Sergeant Smith. "She tried to steal the formula, but Marissa stopped her."

Ellen smirked. "What are we going to do with her?"

Jackson looked at Sergeant Smith. "We're going to fucking kill her."

Rachael stepped in front of Jackson and Sergeant Smith. "We can't. She needs to answer for everything that's happened here. She can't get off that easy."

"Fine. I will tie her up until we finish this."

Rachael grabbed the key for the computer so she could finish the formula.

"You're all stupid. You're throwing away millions," Jessica yelled.

"Yes, maybe. But at least we're not selling our souls for money and power," Rachael replied.

Rachael waved to Ellen. "We have a lot of work still to do if we're going to save some people," she said and then walked back toward the lab.

"Sergeant, you're going to pay when the general gets here. I promise you," Jessica replied. "The people who are coming here don't like failure and have little tolerance for people like you. They will kill everyone here if I don't greet them out there." She snarled menacingly.

Just then, a security officer walked into her office and announced, "We got a message from the general." The officer stopped in his tracks when he saw Jessica tied to the chair and Jackson and Smith standing next to her, and he drew his gun.

"Stand down," Marissa yelled, and he lowered his gun.

"Listen. She didn't tell you what's really going on, did she, or why we are here? There is a horde of infected headed this way, and Rachael, the scientist we brought, can stop it. Jessica here was trying to kill us for the formula." Sergeant Smith's voice was low and he kept his hand out not to startle the young guard.

"Bullshit," the kid replied.

"It's true. Tell him the truth," Marissa said. "The truth is the general was coming, and he was going to take Jessica and leave everyone else here to die."

"So, kid. You with us or not?" Jackson said.

"Untie her now," the guard said. "Not only is she the boss, she's the vice president's wife." His gun was shaking in his hand as he started to slowly walk toward Jessica.

Sergeant Smith moved closer to him. As the kid bent down to untie Jessica, she yelled out, "Watch out."

Before the kid got the gun back around, Sergeant Smith grabbed the gun from him with one hand and punched him with the other, knocking him backward onto the floor.

Marissa walked over to him lying on the ground, her gun in her hand. "You're either with us or against us," she said, putting the gun to his forehead.

The kid started to sweat. He looked up at Marissa and tried to speak, but no words would come out. Sergeant Smith walked over when the kid didn't speak and punched him, knocking him out. "We need to tie him up," he said.

The sergeant looked at Marissa. "Well, Marissa, can you get all your officers on board? We're going to need all their help with what's coming. Also, we have some soldiers on their way here, and we need a radio that can reach them."

"Yes, sir. I will be ready," Marissa replied and walked out of the office.

"You think Captain Miller made it out of the facility?" Jackson asked.

"I hope so, Jackson. We're going to need all the help we can get I fear, even with the antidote."

Jackson looked confused. "Why do you say that?"

"Because if Jessica is telling the truth, we have more reasons to fear the living now than we do the infected. Enough talk. Let's get that radio and see if they made it," Sergeant Smith replied.

Both walked out of the office, leaving Jessica and the kid tied to the chair. Tom followed behind.

Chapter 9

The Escape from the Facility

Brent smiled at Monica. "Hello, Monica. We have a lot to talk about with such little time."

Monica looked up at Brent. The smile made her feel uncomfortable. His face looked like it had twisted itself into that smile. Her voice came out hoarse. "What are you talking about?"

Brent grabbed Monica by the hair and pushed her down in a chair behind a desk. "I'm going to ask you some questions. If I think you're lying, there will be pain," Brent said in a hard tone. "Now, where did everyone go?"

"I don't know."

Brent grabbed Monica's hand and slammed it to the desk. He pulled a knife from his belt and stuck it through her hand, pinning her hand to the desk. Monica let out a scream as blood squirted and the bones in her hand broke.

"Now, you little bitch, where did they go?"

"They went to Eagle's Nest," Monica yelled out in pain, crying.

"Why?"

Still in pain and crying, Monica told Brent about the cure and everything that had happened.

"My good little bitch," Brent said, tapping her face.

"Are you going to kill me?" Monica asked, sniffling.

"Not yet. Now answer my next question. Where did the soldiers go who left on foot?" Brent looked at her with great interest to see if she was lying.

"I told you, Eagle's Nest."

Brent walked behind her and grabbed her other hand, again slamming a knife into her hand and pinning it to the table as well. Monica let out another scream as again bones broke and blood squirted.

"I know they are going to Eagle's Nest. They're not going there on foot. Now where did they go?" Brent pulled out another knife from his belt.

"They're going to their Hummers they left a few miles away." Tears streamed down Monica's face.

Brent grabbed his gun and put his knife away.

"I thought you were not going to kill me?" Monica asked, crying.

"I told you I won't. I'm a man of my word," Brent replied, smiling.

Brent walked over to the computer station, swiped his security card, and pressed the sequence of buttons that would open all doors. As he did so, sirens started to wail in the background.

"I never said I wouldn't leave you to be killed by the infected. Have fun," Brent said.

With that, he sprinted down the hall laughing.

"Don't leave me, please," Monica yelled.

Monica tried to pull her hands free, but she was pinned. She heard an infected coming down the hall.

As Brent left the building out the same side door the captain and his men had used, he heard Monica scream and smiled. "Good riddance, bitch."

Brent tracked the captain and his men, following their footprints up the hill. *Now to settle a different score*, he thought to himself.

Soon, Brent came to a little patch of outpost buildings, where he saw the men gunning down some infected who were stragglers. He watched from a distance.

"Sir, at this rate, we're going to be out of ammo before we reach the Hummers, sir," Dickson said.

"I know it will be close, but we're almost to the Hummers."

As they approached the Hummers, they saw that the doors were open and someone was looking inside one of the vehicles. The captain put up is hand. Everyone came to a halt. He pointed at the Hummers and, with his other hand, gave the signal to move out.

"Don't fucking move," Captain Miller yelled when he had his gun pointed right at the unknown man and Hayes had circled around to the other side, gun raised.

The man, who was wearing military fatigues, put his arms up and slowly came out of the Hummer.

"Who the hell are you?" the captain said, lowering his gun but keeping it ready in case he needed to point it again.

"Colonel Mailey," the man replied, hands still up.

"Where are you from, sir?" Captain Miller said.

"Echo Base," the colonel replied.

"We were at Echo Base. No one was there, sir," Captain Miller said, gun hand beginning to raise as he waited for his answer.

"That's because we were called to go help General Rhodes," the colonel replied.

Turning and looking at his men, Captain Miller then turned back to the colonel. "General Rhodes is dead."

"I'm afraid not, Captain," Colonel Mailey said. He then recounted a tale that played out in his mind as if he were still there.

"Men, get your gear. We're going to Command where General Rhodes is. Get on the chopper now. Move. Move." Putting on headphones, the colonel told the pilot, "Let's go now."

Addressing all the men, he added, "Generals Rhodes is under attack by an unknown enemy. Once we land, we need to secure the base and move to get the general to his evacuation chopper. Then we get back to the chopper for extraction. Do you hear me?"

"Sir, yes, sir," all the men yelled.

Soon, the pilot's voice came over the headphones. "Landing, sir."

"You three, down the ramp first. Secure the landing zone," the colonel shouted.

The men who hit the landing zone were attacked. One of the attackers looked right at the colonel, his face as green as rot and an eye hanging out of its socket, hanging there like a ball on a string. One of the men on the ramp yelled and fired, knocking the thing back. The attacker took a chunk of skin out of his throat. Two other men managed to fight off their attackers, shooting them. The attackers got back up, and one of the men unload his gun into an attacker's chest and stomach, peeling enough skin to see guts pouring out. But the creature still came charging at him. The man behind him shot it in the head, dropping it for good. The third man at the bottom of the ramp saw this and did the same, dropping his relentless attacker.

A medic ran down the ramp to the man down. Checking his pulse, he said solemnly, "He's dead, sir." As the medic looked at the colonel, the soldier awoke and took a chunk out of the medic's hand, sending him flying backward, yelling. Another soldier put a round in his head.

"OK. Just move now. Everyone goes down the ramp to the general's office now." The colonel pointed to two men. "You two, stay here and keep this extraction site clean."

"Yes, sir," they replied.

More attackers came at the men. They all started shooting. Some of them dropped; some kept coming. One of the attackers jumped up, and the colonel saw black ooze coming from its mouth. It ran at one the men, and though it was shot three times in the head, it still jumped on him. Another of the men put his shotgun to its head, exploding it.

Going into the general's office, the colonel saw some of his men dead and others still fighting. "We need to move now, sir."

Escorting him to the chopper, the colonel watched more of his men go down.

The general made it to the chopper. "Get the fuck out of here, Colonel," the general said.

Back at the extraction chopper, the colonel climbed inside, counting only five left out of twenty-five. The back ramp was still open, and the base was on fire now. One of the remaining men, who had been holding his arm, started to shake and then fell down. He immediately jumped up and attacked the pilot. When one of the men grabbed him, pulling him off the pilot, the infected soldier attacked him too, biting his neck and dropping the soldier. The last two men brought the infected soldier to the back of the chopper in an attempt to throw him out, only they wound up going over themselves, along with the infected soldier.

Just as the pilot landed back at Echo Base, the soldier who had been bit in the neck started to get back up.

"I shot him in the head," the colonel said, finishing his story. "Then I helped the pilot out of his seat. He pleaded with me to shoot him, saying, 'I don't want to become one of those things.' I pulled my sidearm and shot him in the head. I gathered myself and just sat for a while, knowing that General Rhodes was behind all of this and knowing that he needs to pay. That's when I remembered sending Dr. Bradley to Acolyte facility. I made my way here."

Captain Miller shook his head. "I can't believe he's still alive."

Dickson heard something behind him. He turned and shots, hitting a young kid in his leg and dropping him.

"Holy shit. It's just a kid, sir," Hayes said.

"If we get him to Eagle's Nest, they can patch him up," Dickson said.

"Fuck that. He's going to slow us down," Hicks replied.

Dickson pushed Hicks. "You're a fucking heartless bastard," he said angrily.

"Me? You're the one who fucking shot him," Hicks said.

"Both of you, shut the fuck up," Captain Miller said. "Dickson's right."

"No, he is too much of a liability. Leave him. We need to move," the colonel said, pulling rank.

"You heard the colonel. Now move. There are people still waiting on us. Drag him into that building and give him some supplies. We need to move to Eagle's Nest," Captain Miller yelled.

Brent watched as the men entered a building and, a few minutes later, exchanged some fire in the building. Brent figured there were more infected inside. *But why go into the building?* he wondered.

He entered the building just as the men he was following exited out the other side. Brent made his way upstairs and saw the boy lying on the ground wrapping his leg. Brent pointed his gun at the boy. "Where are they going?"

"If I tell you, will you take me with you?" the boy asked.

Brent was annoyed. "Yes. Now where?"

"They're going to some place called Eagle's Nest," the boy replied.

"Here. Make yourself useful and grab some explosives and guns. Put them in this bag. I'll fill up this one," Brent said.

As the boy and Brent left the building, Brent asked, "Do you know what way they were headed?"

"Yeah, the only way out of here is Washington Street. Why? They're not friends of yours?" the boy asked.

"Not really. But I need to catch them," Brent replied.

"I know a shortcut. Follow me," the boy replied.

The boy showed Brent a shortcut down an alleyway. "See, I told you. They are just a half a block down that way," the boy said, pointing. "They will have to come up this street to get out of here. So what do we do now?"

"Now, I just need some bait over there by that car. Help me," Brent said.

They worked to push the car into the road.

"What are you going to use as bait? Some of those guns?" the boy asked.

"No. Explosives," Brent said, "and you." He knocked the boy out cold with the butt of his gun and tied him to the car with explosives strapped to him.

As the colonel and the men got out of the Hummers to move some cars in their way, one of the Hummers stopped. It was out of gas.

Brent took one shot at them from the boy's position and quickly got out of view and started working his way around to the Hummers.

"Holy shit. Someone is firing at us, sir," Hicks yelled.

Dickson looked down his scope. "Sir, I got a contact up the hill aways," Dickson said.

"What's he doing, Private? Why hasn't he fired again?" the captain asked.

"Sir, it looks like he's holding a white flag to surrender or something," Dickson said, looking down his scope.

"Captain Miller and Hicks and I will see what he wants. Hayes, get the private's sniper and cover from that tree. Dickson, when I get back, I want this Hummer running," the colonel said.

"Yes, sir," both Dickson and Hayes replied.

Dickson filled the Hummer with gas and primed the engine one time before turning the key. The engine roared to life. He jumped out to close the hood and Brent tapped him on the shoulder. When Dickson turned around, Brent knocked him on his ass and took his weapons.

"Hayes, what is the contact doing?" the captain asked over the radio.

"Still the same, sir. Just standing there," Hayes replied.

As they approach the man. Hicks looked at him. "Holy shit, sir. It's the kid we left, and he's strapped with explosives, sir."

"Dickson, you have the Hummer running? We are leaving now!" the colonel yelled.

"Oh, so soon? You didn't want to stay and see my fireworks." Laughter sounded over the radio.

"Holy shit. That's Brent. How the hell did he know we were here?" Captain Miller said out loud.

The captain and Hayes looked at each other and, at the same time, said, "Monica and Bradley."

Captain Miller grabbed the radio. "How the hell did you get here, Brent? And where are Monica and Bradley?"

"Monica told me. And last I saw her she was waiting on a dinner date, and Bradley lost his mind," Brent said, laughing over the radio.

"You son of a bitch, I'm going to kill you!" Captain Miller yelled.

"Now, I'm going to take this nice Hummer and Dickson here. I got a hot date." Brent started laughing again over the radio.

"How do you think you are going to do that? You will be dead before you get past us?" Hicks yelled over the radio.

"Did you forget I have your friend Dickson here? I will blow his fucking brains out. Got me? Now throw your weapons down and away, all three of you and the sniper in the tree," Brent said.

"Do as he said, now," the colonel said.

Everyone threw their guns away from them.

Just as they did, the boy behind them woke up. "What's going on?" he asked.

"Now release Dickson unharmed," the colonel said.

"I said I wouldn't kill him. I didn't say I wouldn't wound him."

Brent took his knife, jabbed it right through Dickson's leg, and threw him down. Then he jumped into the Hummer and revved the engine.

"Kill that motherfucker," the colonel yelled.

Just as Hicks went for his gun, Brent presses the detonator.

A loud click came from behind the men, and the captain yelled, "Everyone, get down. He's going to explode."

"Who's going to ex—" the boy started to say just before his entire body blew up, sending flesh and bone flying into the air.

With that, Brent drove by laughing.

"We need to go kill that guy now," Hicks yelled.

"Not now. We need to check on Dickson. Hayes, get down here. You have the medical supplies," the colonel ordered.

They got to Dickson and looked at his leg.

"Holy shit. We need to pull that knife out, man," Hicks said.

"No. We first need to make a tourniquet, so he doesn't bleed out when we pull out the knife," Hayes said.

"How do you know that?" Hicks asked.

"I used to be a medic," Hayes replied.

"Hicks, check out the other Hummer and see if we can get it running," Colonel Mailey said.

"I need a belt," Hayes said.

"Here. Take mine," Captain Miller said.

After a few minutes, Hayes had the leg ready, so they could pull out the knife. "We're ready to pull out the knife, but if we don't get to Eagle's Nest soon, he will eventually die," Hayes said. Looking down at Dickson, he added, "This is going to hurt. Ready?"

"Do it," Dickson yelled in pain.

Captain Miller pulled out the knife.

"Hicks, how's the other Hummer?" the colonel yelled.

"It will run, sir. But he took the keys, and with Dickson's leg, we're going to need something bigger to keep the pressure off."

"We're going to be exposed out here, sir. I'm sure that every infected for about a mile in all directions heard that explosion, sir," Captain Miller said.

"Captain Miller, take Hicks and see if you guys can find another vehicle. We need one that's big enough to transfer Dickson."

"Yes, sir."

"Hayes, start dismantling the fifty. We may need it for the next vehicle," the colonel said.

"Yes, sir," Hayes replied.

"I'll stay on watch and let you know if there are any infected."

About twenty minutes went by, and the colonel spotted some incoming infected coming down the hill.

"Hayes, we have incoming. Where the fuck is the captain?" the colonel said.

"Yes, sir," Hayes grabbed his sniper rifle and looked down the scope.

"Shit, sir. There's about twenty coming, sir," Hayes yelled.

"Light them up, Hayes," the colonel said as he opened fire.

Just as they started firing, Captain Miller pulled up in an armored truck.

"Hicks, get out here. Help me with Dickson," the colonel ordered.

"Hurry, sir. More coming." Hayes looked down his scope and fired, taking down another.

Hicks and the colonel got Dickson loaded in the back and pounded on the door. "We're fucking ready. Hayes, get in the fucking truck," Captain Miller yelled.

Hayes grabbed the fifty and threw it in the back of the truck and jumped into the passenger seat. "*Go*!" he yelled.

Captain Miller slammed on the gas and just as the infected arrived. He cut a path straight over the top of them.

"Where the fuck did you guys find this beast?" Hayes asked.

"At a bank. Hicks hot-wired this beast," Captain Miller replied.

Colonel Mailey slid open the little back door in the back of the truck. "What the hell took you so long, Captain?" he asked.

"Sorry, sir. We had to take care of some infected quietly and then had to empty all the money out so Dickson could fit, sir," Captain Miller replied.

"What do we know, sir?" the colonel asked.

"Now, Colonel, we need to get to the Eagle's Nest as quickly as possible and kill that fucking psycho. They don't know he's coming, and we can't contact them because he has the long-range radio."

"Sir, we'll make it. I'm not letting Brent kill Rachael. I promised her that she would be safe, and I'm keeping that promise," Captain Miller said angrily.

"It's General Rhodes. He has the technology that can do this. They've been working on it. I guess it works. It blocks everything except for shortwave radios; that's it," the colonel said.

Miller looked down at his phone and then back up. "Someone had to have filmed some stuff with their iPhone before this technology went up."

"Maybe, but Rhodes has friends in high places. They've probably spun any footage that made it out to be some kind of a hoax or something. The things you can do nowadays. People will believe it. It will show up on some conspiracy sites, I'm sure. But who will believe them?" Colonel Mailey said.

Chapter 10

Arrival of Brent and General Rhodes

Marissa's radio crackled to life as she and Sergeant Smith were looking over the plans for the building, determining how best to defend it from the incoming horde of infected. Meanwhile, Rachael and Ellen finished the batch of the cure and prepared it to be loaded into the plane that Smith and Jackson would take to deliver the cure.

"Marissa come in." The security officer's voice over the radio sounded panicked.

"What is it?" Marissa replied.

"We got a Hummer approaching, ma'am," the security officer said.

"Sergeant, is that your man?" Marissa asked.

"It has to be. That's what we drove to the other facility," Smith said.

"Can you get a hold of them on the radio?" Marissa asked the control room.

"No, ma'am. There has been no answer to the calls to the Hummer," the security officer replied.

"How many men can you have meet us in the entry dock so we can get the captain's help with protecting this base? Jackson and I will hopefully be on our way to release the cure out there on the plane," Sergeant Smith said.

"I have four who can come and help. I need two to stay in the command room and watch the cameras. And I have two greeting the general when he arrives," Marissa said.

"OK. Call and have them meet us there. And have them open the gate," the sergeant said.

He grabbed his radio and called Jackson. "Jackson, how is the cure coming? Has it been loaded inside the plane?"

"Almost there. We have three more canisters to go, and we will be ready for takeoff, sir. Why? Is something wrong?" Jackson said.

"No, the captain and the others are just arriving. I'm going to meet them in the bay now," the sergeant said.

"Do you need me to come down there, sir?" Jackson asked.

"No. Just make sure Rachael is finishing that cure as fast as possible. We don't have much time. I'm sure the captain saw the horde on the way in," Sergeant Smith said.

"I'll make sure it's ready, sir. Over and out," Jackson replied.

Marissa and her men, along with Sergeant Smith, were standing on the arrival dock as the Hummer pulled in through the gate and stopped a few feet away. "Hey, guys. Long time no see," the sergeant yelled.

"Are you sure that's them, Sergeant?" Marissa asked, grabbing her gun.

"I don't know. Something strange is going on," Smith replied.

In one smooth motion, a person popped out of the hole on the roof of the Hummer and started firing the fifty at the men at the top of the docks. The first few shots ripped through the first guard, turning his body into Swiss cheese. The second guard tried to jump behind some boxes, but the bullets tore through his legs, blowing them off completely. The other two guards managed to get behind the boxes before the volley of shots got to them. Smith grabbed Marissa just in time to throw her into the hallway.

"What the fuck is going on?" Marissa yelled at the sergeant.

"Holy fuck! It's Brent. How the fuck did he know where we went?" Smith said.

"Brent? Who the hell is Brent?" Marissa yelled.

"You need to get the rest of your men and find Rachael," Smith yelled.

"Rachael? What's going on?" Marissa yelled back.

"No time. Just please do as I ask," the sergeant said in an angry tone.

"But my men are still in there," Marissa replied.

"I will see if I can help them. Just go, please, now," Smith yelled once again.

Marissa hurried the other way down the hall.

Smith got close to the door, hoping for a good vantage point. He saw that two of the men were down, one dead for sure. The other was bleeding profusely, and he was missing both legs. The remaining two huddled behind some boxes, scared to death. Smith waved for them to come for the door. They shook their heads, stiff and scared to move.

Smith yelled to Brent, "Brent, how the hell did you find us?"

"Had help from some of your friends. I'm here to see the doctor. Know where she is?" Brent said, laughing.

Smith barely had enough time to get out of the way before shots sprayed the wall by him.

"Hey, guys behind the boxes, if you get out now, I won't kill you. Promise. OK, how about Scout's honor?" Brent said.

"You won't kill us?" one of the guards yelled back.

"Don't listen to him. He's crazy," Sergeant Smith yelled.

"My beef is with the guy over there. If you leave now, I will not kill you," Brent yelled.

"OK, I'm coming out," one of the guards called out.

"Don't do it!" the sergeant warned.

The guard got up and started walking toward the door. Brent pressed the trigger and held it down, sending shot after shot straight through the guard until almost nothing was left of him, and the fifty ran dry.

"Did I forget to mention I was never in the Scouts?" Brent said, laughing.

The sergeant heard the gun go dry. He ran around the corner and fired his weapon at Brent, just missing his head. "You crazy motherfucker, now you're trapped. Your gun's out," he yelled, firing at the Hummer.

Now, the remaining guard stood up, firing as well.

Both Smith and the guard stopped firing. "Fucking come out now, Brent, so I can kill you where you are fucking stand," Smith says angrily.

"Guess again," Brent yelled and stepped out of the Hummer with a rocket launcher. He fired.

"Holy shit!" The sergeant ran toward the door, the guard in tow.

Just as the sergeant made it through the door, the rocket exploded, sending him and the guard backward. The blast killed the guard, and some metal from the explosion cut into the sergeant's arm.

His radio came to life with Jackson on the other end. "What the hell was that? It shook the entire facility," Jackson said.

"It's Brent, and he has an entire arsenal with him. He just blew up one of the doors at the entrance," the sergeant replied.

"Are you OK, sir?" Jackson asked worriedly.

"Yes. Is the plane loaded?" the sergeant asked.

"Almost. One more container, sir," Jackson replied.

"Good. Finish up and get the plane ready and get my son on board," the sergeant ordered.

The sergeant switched the radio to Marissa's frequency. "Marissa, do you copy?"

"Yes, Sergeant. Is everything OK? That explosion shook everything," Marissa said.

"Yes, I'm fine. But your guards are dead. He blew one of the doors up where we were standing. Is there another way out of the docks?" he asked urgently.

"All of them are dead? I will kill him." Her voice cracked as she held back tears. "Yes. The other door goes to the labs. I'm here with Rachael now. She has the last container ready. And the general will be here in less than five minutes, Sergeant. Maybe he can deal with Brent. He said he has about fifteen soldiers with him."

"Well, you will have to get in line. OK. On my way to you. Hold tight," Smith said and ran down the hall in the direction she'd guided him.

Brent got up off the floor. He'd been knocked back by the force of the blast. Grabbing the other weapons he'd stored in the Hummer, he walked over to the map of the facility on the wall to determine where the control room was. He looked over and, seeing an intercom on the wall, pressed a button.

"Honey, I'm home. Don't worry. I'll see you in a bit." Brent laughed loudly.

In the labs, the scientists were still working. John stopped and looked at his fellow researcher, Ryan. "Did you hear that? It sounded like there were gunshots."

"It's probably another stupid drill," Ryan started to say. But he stopped in midsentence when they both heard what very much sounded like an explosion.

Next, a voice sounded over the intercom. Whoever had announced that he was "home," followed by a peal of laughter, sounded more than just a little deranged.

John grabbed the phone and dialed for security, but no one answered. "I don't like this. I think we need to get out of here."

Just then, John saw someone walking down the hall. Thinking it was one of the men whose arrival they had been briefed about, John and Ryan run out into the hall.

Ryan looked at the man walking passed them. "Hey, did you hear that explosion? What's going on?" He sounded unsure.

Brent stopped in his tracks and turned to looks at the two men in lab coats. He shot them both and kept walking down the hall. Other people saw this and started running for other exits.

Ellen and Rachael and Marissa saw a group of scared-looking scientists running down the hall from the other labs on the other side of the facility. Marissa stopped one of them. "What happened? Why are you running?" she asked.

"There was a man heading toward the control room, and he killed John and Ryan, just shot them," Carrol said in a panic.

"Carrol, get Bruce and Adam in this lab. They will be safe here," Marissa said.

"Where are all the security officers, ma'am?" Carrol asked.

"There are some marines coming, and they will be able to help. Just get in the lab," Marissa said impatiently.

"They're dead, aren't they? Mark, Clint, and David are all dead," Carrol said crying.

"Carrol, I know you're scared. Just please get in the lab now."

Marissa, seeing that Carrol was breaking down even more, gently guided her into the lab. The other scientists joined her.

Just then, Sergeant Smith finally burst into the lab, his arm bleeding heavily. Rachael saw this and ran over and grabbed him.

"Sergeant, are you all right?" Rachael asked.

"It's just a scratch," Sergeant Smith said.

"Let's look at this scratch," Rachael said.

Rachael lifted his sleeve and saw the metal stuck through his arm. She hurried him to a lab station and called for Ellen and Marissa's help.

Marissa's radio comes to life. "Ma'am, the general's chopper is touching down now," a guard said.

"Thank you. Please lead him to Jessica Price's office," Marissa replied. "Control room, please come in," she said over the radio.

"Control room here. Go ahead, ma'am," another guard replied.

"Do you still have eyes on the intruder?" Marissa asked.

"No, ma'am. He destroyed most of the cameras, and I haven't seen him since the lab, ma'am," the guard replied.

"Just to let you know, some of the doctors said he was headed your way. So be ready," Marissa said.

"One other thing. There's another truck approaching, an armored truck, and they're plowing right through a horde of infected, ma'am," the guard said.

"Sergeant, did you hear that? Can you get a hold of them on your radio now?" Marissa asked.

"I'll try," the sergeant replied.

"Captain Miller, do you read me?" the sergeant said over the radio.

"Yes, Sergeant. This is Captain Miller. Sorry we're late."

"That's all right, sir. It's good to hear your voice," the sergeant replied.

"Did Brent already get there, Sergeant?" Captain Miller asked.

"Yes, sir. And he's already made a mess of everything, sir," the sergeant replied.

"Sorry about that, Sergeant. He caught us off guard and stole the Hummer. Can you get that gate down? We are coming in fast," the captain said.

"Yes, sir," the sergeant replied.

"Ma'am, there is a doctor outside the control room screaming for help," the guard said.

"Do not open that door, do you hear me? We need control of that room at all costs," Marissa said.

Blain stared nervously at the monitor. The noiseless black and white image of a woman in a lab coat pounded frantically on the door. "Chief, it's Sheri, I mean, Dr. Omari. Should I let her in?"

Omari, fuck. They'd gone to a couple of cooking classes together—French fusion. She didn't want to condemn the genial woman to death, but her hands were tied. "Do not open that door under any circumstances."

Blain's mouth felt open. "But, I mean, Christ, we've gone on a couple of dates, and—"

Jordan rose and towered over Blain. "You heard the chief. Drop it."

Blain looked back at the screen. "Fuck this," he muttered under his breath.

He leaped up, catching Jordan by surprise, and knocked the bigger man off balance.

Jordan stumbled two steps and fell back into a chair. "Shit, no. Blain, you idiot." Jordan grabbed for him, but it was too late. Blain was already past him.

Blain punched in the code and yanked the door wide open.

As soon as the door opened, Brent shot Blain, knocking him backward into the security room. Jordan put his hand up. The radio was still squawking with Marissa's voice.

"Hey, man, you can have the security room," Jordan said, looking down at his friend. But any thoughts of revenge going through his mind were stomped out upon seeing Brent holding the gun.

"Yeah, you can go," Brent said.

Jordan turned around and ran. Just as he got to the door, Brent shot him in the back. "I said you could go; I didn't say how far," Brent said, laughing.

"Control, can you please open the gate for the truck?" Marissa said over the radio.

"I'm sorry. I gave your guards a break indefinitely," Brent said, laughing.

"You son of a bitch," Marissa screamed back over the radio.

Brent switched frequencies and started to talk to the truck. "Hello. This is control. I'm sorry. The gate will not be open at this time," Brent said, laughing maniacally.

"What the hell? Is that you, Brent?" Hayes asked.

The captain ignored Smith and yelled to the men in the back, "Hang on. We're going to have to make our own gate." Captain Miller pushed harder on the gas as he continued to plow through the infected. Finally clear of the horde, he pushed even harder on the gas, making the truck go as fast as possible.

"Captain, that horde is following us, If we make a hole, they will get in," Hayes said.

"We will get the explosives in the back and blow up this truck, sealing the entrance," Captain Miller replied.

Brent, watching the cameras, saw the huge helicopter touch down. A general and ten marines got out of the chopper. The two guards waiting for the general ran up to him.

"Hello, General," one of the guards said. "Thank God you're here."

"Where is Mrs. Price?" General Rhodes asked.

"She's in her office with Marissa, sir," the guard replied.

"What are you guys going to do about the infected heading this way?" asked another guard, a little bit of panic in his voice.

"Don't worry about that. We're here to help and relieve you gentlemen. We will handle it from here. Both of you did a good job," the general said.

The general called over to the captain of the marine unit accompanying him. "Captain, you want to relieve these men," the general said.

"No problem, sir," the captain replied. He quickly drew his sidearm and shot both guards in the head.

General Rhodes yelled back toward the chopper, "Vice President Price, sir, we're all clear here, sir."

Vice President Don Price walked out of the chopper. He was a man who carried a look of confidence. With his blond hair and very stocky build, his wasn't what you would consider an average look for a vice president. As he came out of the chopper, his command was smooth and without question. His political career had started when he was very young, and he'd learned from powerful friends where and how to make trouble for his rivals in the political arena. His wife, half politician, half researcher, shared his views. She helped him in his career. Like chess pieces, they helped each other, crushing anyone in their path. Once he was vice president, he got her the position of head researcher at a top facility. Once there, they had a plan that would take them all the way to the top. "General, let's get this over with."

"Captain Fields, go in and round up all the scientists and relieve them of their posts as well," General Rhodes said.

"Yes, sir," Captain Fields replied. "Let's move out now," he yelled to the marines.

And they all walked inside.

Brent shut off the camera to the outside chopper pad and grinned. "Now, this is going to be fun," he said to himself.

Grabbing his guns and knives, he walked out of the control room whistling.

Chapter 11

Sacrifice and Betrayal

Hayes, who had just taken the wheel from the captain, drove the armored truck through the first gate and yelled to the men in the back, "Brace yourselves."

The truck slammed into the garage gate, bursting through and then stopping almost instantly—making everyone slam into the front of the truck.

"Set up the fifty and grab the explosives," the colonel said.

Captain Miller got on the fifty in the back of the truck.

"Get me up. I will man the fifty while you guys set up the explosives," Dickson said.

Hicks and the colonel stood Dickson on his feet and placed him by the fifty. Looking out at the back of the building, Dickson saw what looked like a cloud, but he knew it was a horde of infected heading this way.

"Are you sure you're good, man? How's your leg?" Hicks asked, looking down at his leg where Brent had stabbed him. Blood soaked through the dressing they'd applied, and Hicks thought it looked concerning.

"I'm good. Leg is fine. Start setting up the explosives," Dickson replied.

"Captain, take the lieutenant and secure the garage. Hicks and I will finish the explosives," the colonel said.

"Incoming!" Dickson yelled and started firing the fifty, taking down the first wave of infected.

Captain Miller and Lieutenant Hayes finished their sweep of the garage and headed back to the colonel. "Sir, four guards dead. Looks like

Brent caught them off guard, sir. The door on the right looks like it was taken out by a rocket," Captain Miller said.

"All explosives set, sir," Hicks said.

"Hicks, grab Dickson and meet us by the door," the colonel said.

Hicks ran over to Dickson, who was still firing the fifty. "Let's go, man," Hicks said.

"No. I will just slow all of you down," Dickson replied.

"Get the fuck off that gun, Private," Hicks yelled back.

"Look," Dickson pointed out, "the horde is coming. By the time you help me down, they will be here. Just give me the detonator and get the fuck out of here please. Look, I lost too much blood anyway. I can barely stand. Just go," Dickson said.

Hicks handed Dickson the detonator, at first hesitantly. Then he called, "Give 'em hell," and ran for the door.

Dickson fired the fifty again as the horde approached, now moving even faster. And he could see there were hundreds this time. The horde hit the truck hard, knocking Dickson off the gun and to the back of the truck. In the blink of an eye, the horde had jumped on him, clawing and biting. Dickson, with detonator in hand, yelled, "Eat this, motherfuckers." He pressed the button.

Hicks ran through the door to the labs, meeting up with the others.

"Where's Dickson?" Captain Miller asked.

"He held off the horde so I could get away," Hicks replied.

"We need to help him," Lieutenant Hayes yelled.

As soon as the words left his mouth, a huge explosion shook the facility. Hayes grabbed Hicks. "You left him, didn't you?" he demanded.

"You think I wanted to? He wanted to stay for us, for the cause. And he knew that if I tried helping him, we would both die. So, he made the choice, not me. I would have stayed till the end," Hicks replied, shoving the lieutenant back.

"Enough, both of you. We need to find Sergeant Smith and Jackson to see if they need help. Remember, that fucking asshole Brent is in here somewhere. So, grab your shit. We will have time to mourn our man later," the captain said.

"Yes, sir," both Hicks and Hayes replied.

Jackson, Smith, and Tom were waiting in the labs when some military guys came in and started shoving the scientists, telling them not to move.

Sergeant Smith and Jackson ducked behind some boxes in the connecting hallway, pulling Tom along with them. From there, they could see a man they recognized as the vice president. It seemed it was his men who were pushing the scientists, Carrol, Adams, and Bruce, around. Sergeant Smith watched General Rhodes come around the corner last. "Holy shit. That's General Rhodes," the sergeant said under his breath.

"That's General Rhodes," Jackson hissed.

"Looks good for a dead man," Sergeant Smith said, staring at him, recalling that the last time he'd seen the general was at forward base falling to a swarm of infected.

"From the base we were at, what the hell are they doing here?"

"What do you want to do? Why are they shoving the scientists?" Jackson said.

"Hold your position, Private. Son, get down and stay down," the sergeant said.

At that moment, a huge explosion shook everything.

"What the hell was that?" Jackson asked.

"That was the captain and the others. I'm sure of it. Stay here and wait for support. They should be here soon," the sergeant said.

Vice President Price and General Rhodes walked into the main office and saw Jessica tied to her chair and gagged. Rachael, Ellen, and Marissa stood beside her, waiting.

"Well, Jessica, you really fucked this up, now didn't you? The president asked for me to take care of you personally," Vice President Price said. He walked over to her tied to the chair and got down to look her right in the eyes.

"Sir, I'm sorry we had to tie her up with the help of some of the marines. She tried to take the formula by force, and we had to make sure she didn't hurt anyone," Ellen said.

"Well, Ellen, she was supposed to do that and bring me Rachael over there," Vice President Price said. Standing up straight again, he turned from looking at Jessica and now looked right at Ellen.

"*What*?" Ellen said, shocked.

Just as he said that, the general pulled out his gun and pointed it at all three women.

When they were distracted by a huge explosion, Ellen tried grabbing the gun. "Run, Rachael," she yelled out.

Rachael ran out the door and down the hallway toward the labs.

The general quickly shook Ellen off and pointed the gun once more at Marissa and Ellen.

"Try that again and I will kill you," General Rhodes said to Ellen.

The general quickly grabbed his radio and called for his captain. "What was that explosion?"

"I'm not sure, sir," Captain Fields replied.

"Maybe you need to go find out. Also, a scientist is coming your way. Intercept her and bring her back unharmed, Captain," the general said.

"Yes, sir. I will bring her to you and send some men to find out about that explosion, sir," the captain replied.

The captain sent three men toward the explosion. Then he saw a woman running down the hall toward the lab. He sent his men in pursuit, following close behind.

"Holy shit. There's Rachael" Jackson said, still hiding behind some cabinets. "What do you want to do, sir?" Jackson asked Smith.

"There are too many of them, Private. We have to wait for Captain Miller and the others to help her," Smith replied.

As three men approached the exit to the lab, Brent jumped out, stabbing the first man in the eye and killing him. Without missing a step, he threw his other knife, killing the second man and then quickly pulled his gun on the third. "Move," Brent said, pressing the gun to the marine's back.

Brent approached another group of marines, all of whom had their guns on him.

"Let him go," one marine yelled.

Then the captain of the marines walked over. "What do you want?" Captain Fields asked.

"I'll trade you the marine for that scientist," Brent said, pointing at Rachael.

"I can't do that. Take one of the others," the captain said, pointing to the other scientist, Carrol.

"I don't want them," Brent said as he pointed his gun and started firing into the scientists standing by him, killing Carrol.

"I can't. It's not my call. Come and talk to the general. Follow me," the captain said, walking toward the main office.

"Fine," Brent said, still holding the gun to the back of the marine as he followed Captain Fields.

Jackson and Smith looked over the cabinets where some of the scientists lay dead on the ground. "We have to do something," Jackson said, pleading with Smith.

"Not yet, Private," Smith replied.

"If we don't, they're all going to die, sir," Jackson said.

"I will not risk my son for those scientists," Smith replied.

"Sergeant, Brent is following the other marine, sir. They are also taking Rachael with them. I think they're going to the back office," Jackson said.

"Sir, you might want to get up here," Hicks said, bending over to check the pulses of some marines on the floor, who were, as he guessed, dead.

"What is it, Hicks?" Captain Miller said.

Hicks rolled one of the men over. "There are dead marines here, sir. Both stab wounds to the head."

"Sir, we have a situation here, sir," Lieutenant Hayes said as he looked down his scope.

"What is it, Lieutenant?" Colonel Mailey asked.

"I have eight marines and two scientists, and one of the marines just put a round into one of the scientist's heads, sir," Hayes replied.

"Take him out, Lieutenant," the colonel said.

Hayes lined up his shot and put a round right through the marine's head. As soon as he dropped, the other marines took cover and started to return fire. Captain Miller, Hicks, and the colonel took cover and returned fire. Two more marines went down. The scientists got up and tried to run but were cut down by the marines.

"We need to flank them, or Captain Miller and the others are going to get pinned down," Sergeant Smith said.

Jackson and Sergeant Smith snuck around behind the marines and fired, taking down the last three marines. The firing stopped. The sergeant yelled to Captain Miller, "All clear."

Captain Miller came out from the labs and saw Sergeant Smith and Jackson standing there.

"Sergeant, report," the captain said.

"Well, sir, a couple of marines took Brent and Rachael to the back offices, and General Rhodes is alive, sir," Sergeant Smith said.

"We know. Meet Colonel Mailey. He told us that," Captain Miller said.

Sergeant Smith nodded to the colonel.

"And the fucking vice president is there, too," Jackson blurted out.

"What? Are you serious?" Hicks replied out loud.

"Yes, sir," Jackson said. "He's back there with General Rhodes."

"If Rhodes is here, then he wants the cure. Is it ready to go?" Captain Miller asked.

"Sir, the plane is loaded and ready to go. We just need the key for the doors and the security officer, who is also back with them," Sergeant Smith replied.

"Sir, if Brent went back there, I'm not sure what he was up to. He killed all the security officers here and most of the scientists. I promised Rachael that she'd be safe. We need to get her out of there," Sergeant Smith said.

"What the hell is the vice president doing here?" the colonel asked.

"Not sure, sir. I think they're after the cure. Jessica Price wanted the cure. She wanted to kill all of us for it, so we tied her up in those offices. He could be here for her as well," Sergeant Smith explained.

"Why kill all the scientists?" Captain Miller asked.

"Sir, I think they're trying to cover this up," Sergeant Smith replied.

"All right. Listen up. Hicks, Sergeant Smith, and Jackson, stay here. Secure the area and watch his son. The captain, the lieutenant, and I will go and help Rachael," the colonel said.

"Wait, where the hell is Dickson?" the sergeant asked.

"Fucking Brent killed him. He's going to pay with his life," Hicks said, scowling in anger.

Brent, Rachael, and the two marines walked into the back office. They overheard the vice president talking to Jessica, saying he should kill her or leave her here to die for her failure. The vice president turned to meet the men entering.

"Ahh, thank you, Rachael, for returning to us," he said.

"Fuck you, sir. I will not give you the cure," Rachael replied.

"We'll see. And who is this?" the vice president said, pointing to Brent.

"His name is Brent, sir. Says he wants Rachael, here," Captain Fields said.

Brent stepped out from behind the marine, still keeping his gun trained on the man. "Yes, Mr. Vice President, I want Rachael. She is mine," Brent said.

"How about you lower that gun, and we can talk?" the vice president said.

Brent lowered his weapon and walked over to the vice president, offering his hand. "So, you got a name? Or do I just call you Vice President?" he said.

"Vice President is fine. Now, tell me, why do you need Rachael? What is she to you?"

"She left me to die, and I am going to kill her," Brent said, grinning.

"Well," Price began slowly, "I admit that it sounds like she did you a grievous wrong."

"Damn straight," Brent replied.

Price held up a finger. "But." His voice dragged out the word. "It is not within my power to remand her into your custody. I'm afraid she's vital to our national security. As a patriotic American, I'm sure you can understand that."

The moment Price was done talking, Captain Fields pointed his gun at Brent. "Let's go. Move to the hallway."

Just then, gunfire erupted from the labs. Brent took advantage of the captain's distraction. He pulled his knife and stabbed him in the head and then whipped around, grabbing his gun in the same motion, and shot the other marine who was escorting him in the head. Next, he fired at the general, who jumped through the back door, catching a round in the shoulder. Then Brent turned the gun toward Rachael, Marissa, and Ellen. "Anyone else moves, and I will fucking kill you all."

"He's serious," Rachael said, scared.

Brent walked over and grabbed the vice president by the neck and pressed the gun to his head. "So, what's your name? I think we are there now, don't you?"

"It's Don," the vice president said, without even flinching.

"Well, Don, who do we have here tied up?" Brent asked, dragging Don over to the chair.

"This is Jessica, my wife," Don said.

Brent walked over to one of the dead marines and pulled his gun from his belt. With one hand, he pulled out the clip and emptied it, leaving one round in the chamber. He handed it to the vice president. "Go over and shoot Jessica in the head," Brent said.

"No. I was just saying that to scare her. I would never kill my wife," Don said, holding the gun in his hand. Sweat was now pouring off his brow.

"All right. I will show you how to follow through with what you say," Brent said.

Brent walked over and grabbed one of the girls sitting next to Rachael, pulling her up off the floor. "What's your name?" Brent asked.

"Ellen," Ellen said.

"OK, Don. You have three seconds to shoot your wife," Brent said.

"I can't," Don said, his composure now starting to dwindle. He was sweating all over.

"Oh, come on, Don. You want to be president. One. Come on, Don. Her death is going to be on you, Don. Two." Brent laughed gleefully.

"Please, Brent. You win. If you're trying to scare me, man, you win. I'll give you whatever you want," Don said, now contrite.

"Three," Brent said.

Brent pulled the trigger, shooting Ellen in the head and making Don jump. Rachael and Marissa looked away.

"Looks like you just lost a voter. I told you, Don. Now that's how you follow through with what you say. Now the pressure's really on, because it's you or your wife. One of you will die in three seconds. I shoot you if you don't shoot your wife," Brent said, smiling.

Don closed his eyes and composed himself. He lifted the gun, but instead of pointing it at Jessica, he pointed it right at Brent. "Here's how it's going to go. You are going to let my wife and Rachael leave. Or you're going to die. Got that?" Don's words sounded strong and forceful.

"Finally, you found your balls, Don. I like it. You only have one shot. Don't miss," Brent said, laughing.

Don's hand started to shake as he realized he'd never actually shot anyone. Brent, seeing the strength leave his eyes, quickly knocked the gun from his hand and pointed his gun right into his face. "You had your chance. Now I'm going to show you how to do it," Brent said.

"You sick fucking bastard," Rachael yelled.

"Don't worry, Rachael. Your time is coming," Brent said, looking right into Don's eyes.

Just before he could pull the trigger, someone slammed into him, making the gun go off, and a round slammed into Don's leg.

Brent looked up to see the colonel on top of him, punching him.

Captain Miller rushed into the room right after the colonel and grabbed Rachael and Marissa.

"What about Jessica? We can't just leave her," Rachael said.

Captain Miller ran over and untied Jessica as the colonel and Brent continued fighting. "Let's go," Captain Miller yelled to them.

"The general got away. We need to find him before he gets away," Rachael said.

"I'll find him," Marissa said.

"No. I need you to get my men to the plane, so we can get that cure in the air. Rachael and I will find him. Go with the sergeant and get them to the plane," Captain Miller said.

Marissa and the sergeant ran back to meet the other men waiting in the labs.

"Come on," the sergeant called, waving to the others. "Marissa has the key. Move."

Together, they ran toward the back door, where Marissa was already waiting.

"There are a few infected out there. We need to move fast and get everyone on the plane," Marissa said.

"Wait. We all have the cure. You don't. Best if you give me your badge, and we can take it from here," the sergeant said.

Marissa handed him her badge to open the security doors. "Good luck, Sergeant. Can you give me a gun? I will help if I can," Marissa said.

The sergeant handed her one of the rifles. "We will drop the cure and be back," he said.

"Hicks, when I open this door, you're on point. Drop any infected. If you can't hit their heads, go for the legs. Bring them down. The rest of us will be behind you covering your advance. When you get to the plane, open the door and cover us while we get inside," the sergeant said.

Sergeant Smith opened the door, and Hicks was the first one out. He immediately fired at some infected who heard the door open, taking all three down with clean headshots. The other three men, along with the sergeant and his son, moved toward the runway also firing. Hicks got to the plane first and opened the doors and turned just as the sergeant told him to.

"Come on," Hicks yelled, shooting another infected.

As the men reached the plane, it seemed like an endless wave of infected was coming. The sergeant helped first his son on board and then Jackson. "Jackson, get her ready to go now," he yelled.

As Lieutenant Hayes was getting in the plane, the sergeant stopped frozen like a statue as he looked at the name on Marissa's ID badge. It read, "Marissa Rhodes." Hicks, still firing on the infected, was yelling for him to get on the plane.

"Jackson," the sergeant said, "take off. Get that cure on the ground now. Keep as low as possible. If the government has set up quarantines, they will shoot you down. You got only one shot at this."

"What? Where are you going?" Jackson said.

"I need to get back inside," the sergeant said.

"Dad, I want to go with you," Tom cried.

"Stay here. This is going to be the safest place for you," the sergeant said.

Before Jackson could say another word, the sergeant sprinted toward the building. Hicks was still laying down covering fire.

"What the fuck we do now?" Lieutenant Hayes yelled.

"We do what he asked. Get in the copilot seat. Let's get this thing in the air and save some people. Hicks, close the door," Jackson said.

Hicks closed the door and gave him a thumbs-up, and Jackson started the plane and got in the air.

After jumping on Brent, the colonel kept throwing punches to Brent's face, staying on top of the younger man. Brent caught one of the colonel's punches and managed to wedge his leg against the colonel's chest. Using that leverage, he pushed the colonel off and to the floor.

Brent and the colonel got to their feet, facing each other, ready for the next round.

Brent spat what looked like black ooze out of his mouth. "You hit like a bitch," he said, wiping his mouth.

The colonel launched another attack, but this time, Brent was ready. He caught the colonel's right hand and connected with an uppercut to the colonel's jaw and a front kick to the colonel's chest, knocking him to the ground.

The colonel picked himself off the ground, rubbing his jaw. "I'm going to kill you, Brent, for Dickson and the others, you piece of shit," Colonel Mailey said, getting into battle stance.

"Come get your revenge if you can, bitch," Brent replied.

The colonel attacked again, this time landing a punch to Brent's stomach and a left to his head that sent him backward. The colonel pressed his assault with a kick to Brent's head. Brent caught his foot and swept his leg, sending the colonel to the floor again. With the colonel on the ground, Brent landed a kick to his ribs, hearing a bone crack in the colonel's chest.

With the colonel on the ground holding his ribs, Brent pulled a knife from his belt. "Now I'm going to kill you and then your friends," he said.

While the colonel and Brent had been fighting, Don had gotten up and limped out of the room. When he saw Marissa coming, he ducked behind some boxes, waiting till she passed and then making his way to his choppers.

When Marissa got back to Rachael's office, she saw Brent kicking the colonel, who lay on the ground. She took the opportunity to land a kick of her own, knocking Brent back.

Brent's eyes went wide when he saw Marissa standing there holding a gun right at him.

"This is for all my men you killed, you son of a bitch," Marissa yelled stitching four rounds across Brent's chest, making him fly over a chair to the ground.

The colonel got up, still holding his ribs, and Marissa trained the gun on him. "I was going to say thank you, but it looks like you're not going to accept it," the colonel said, still holding his ribs.

"Shut up and listen. My father is General Rhodes. He's going to kill thousands, maybe even millions. I know this because he wanted me to come in on his plan, and I just can't do it. I don't know if I can trust you."

"Why do you say that?" the colonel asked, one hand still on his side.

"Because you're wearing one of his patches for the Raven Squadron," Marissa replied.

"Used to be with that squadron, ma'am. Your father has to pay. All my men are dead, and he will answer for it one way or another." The colonel reached for the patch and pulled it off in one quick motion.

"Then you will help me stop him," Marissa said, putting down her gun.

"I will be glad to."

They turned around and left the room to find Captain Miller and Rachael.

Captain Miller and Rachael ran down the hall. When Rachael stopped, so did Captain Miller. Giving her a puzzled expression, he asked, "What are you doing?"

"Where the hell did Jessica go? She was right behind us? She's going to get away." Rachael sounded angry.

"We will find her. Right now, we have to stop Rhodes. He's the bigger threat right now."

"I agree. But if she escapes, she can cover everything up. She has just as powerful friends as the general." Rachael met the captain's gaze.

"I promise she will pay," Captain Miller said.

With that, they turned and ran together down the hall.

Vice President Don Price got out to the landing pad and started to limp his way up the ramp of his chopper, his leg still bleeding. As he went to close the hatch, he looked up to see a gun in his face. On the other end of the weapon was Jessica Price.

"Honey, what the hell are you doing?" Don said.

"Something I should have done a long time ago," Jessica said and shot Don in the head.

Closing the hatch, Jessica yelled at the pilot to get the chopper going. The pilot, afraid of being killed, took off in a hurry. Jessica picked up the phone Rhodes had given her. "I have the cure. I'm on my way to you," she said simply and then hung up.

Brent woke up and looked down at his chest to see the black ooze coming from the bullet holes just like he'd seen before. And once more, his wounds were already starting to heal.

"That little bitch is going to pay," he said to himself. Getting to his feet, he grabbed his gun off the floor and stormed out of the office.

Chapter 12
The General's Plan

Rachael and Captain Miller walked into another office, Captain Miller with his gun raised. On the other end was General Rhodes, who was on the phone.

"Hang up the phone now," Captain Miller yelled, gun in hand.

The general hung up the phone and scooted back from the desk.

"Who were you on the phone with?" Captain Miller asked.

"I was on the line with some of my men," the general said.

"Are they coming here?" Captain Miller asked.

"No," the general said.

"He's lying," Rachael said.

"I have no reason to lie to you. I told them to continue with the mission at hand, whether I meet them or not," the general said.

"What mission?" Captain Miller asked, still holding the gun on him.

Before the general could answer, Marissa and Colonel Mailey walked into the room, guns pointed at the general as well.

"Did they get on the plane?" Rachael asked Marissa.

"Yes, they did and should be dispensing the cure as we speak," Marissa replied.

"Good. The general doesn't want to tell us who was on the phone—something about a mission," Captain Miller reported.

Before anyone else could speak, Colonel Mailey, with his rifle pointed right at the general, roared, "You remember me, you son of a bitch?"

The general looked at him, and his eyes widened for a second before he quickly regained his composure. "Yes," he said. "You are the one who got me out of the base."

"I lost all of my men because of you. And now you are going to pay," the colonel said, trying to keep his feelings from overtaking him.

"Colonel, you need to calm down. We need him alive," Captain Miller said, stepping in front of the colonel.

"Please, Colonel. He's my father. Don't hurt him, and I will tell you the plan," Marissa said, fear in her voice.

Everyone turned and looked at Marissa, who had turned her gun on the colonel.

"I know you don't want to hear this, Colonel. But your men were expendable assets. If they didn't die there, it was just a matter of time. I gave them a mercy killing really," the general said with a little chuckle.

The colonel pushed Captain Miller to the side and punched the general in the face.

"My men are not expendable, you piece of shit," the colonel said as Captain Miller pushed him backward.

Marissa grabbed Rachael and pointed the gun at her. "Let us go, and I will tell you what you want to know. I didn't want anything to do with his plans, but he is my father." Marissa stared at the colonel and Captain Miller.

"You fucking bitch," Rachael said, trying to squirm away.

"Why are you doing this, Marissa? You're not like him," Captain Miller said.

Before she could answer, the general cut in. "Why? It comes down to power," he said.

"Power? It's just a cure for Compound Z, and that has been all destroyed. And as soon as they dump the cure, there will not be any need for that," Rachael explained.

"True. But if I have someone who is already infected could spread it again, then the country who has the cure has the power," the general said.

"What the hell have you done?" Rachael said angrily.

"Let's just say after today the United States will be the most powerful, and other countries will give anything for this cure," the general said with a smirk.

Sergeant Smith, who had been listening from just outside the door, slipped into the room a few feet behind Marissa and drew his gun on her.

Marissa quickly turned, moving Rachael with her, and pointed her gun at Sergeant Smith.

"I trusted you, Marissa. I trusted you," Sergeant Smith said.

Marissa's radio crackled to life. On the other end was Jackson.

"All the cure is gone; it looks like it's working. A lot of the infected are already dying. And hopefully, we saved some people. We're on our way back," Jackson reported.

The sergeant walked toward Marissa slowly. "You're not like them," he said. "I can tell you were deeply hurt by the death of your men at Brent's hand. You cared for them. You can't let your father go. We have to stop him. You know that."

Marissa lowered her gun.

Captain Miller turned and looked at the general. "Now make the call and tell your men to stand down." Slamming his hands in fists on the table, he leaned in, staring at the general.

"Or what?" The general's tone was mocking. "You have nothing to bargain with. And just in case you're thinking you could threaten me with my daughter, you don't have it in you. But just to make sure." He pulled his sidearm and shot his daughter.

Marissa's eyes went wide, and she fell to the ground.

"Now you have nothing," General Rhodes said.

Rachael went to Marissa and tried to put pressure on her wound.

Just then, Brent walked into the room. "Now that's some straight-up villain shit," he said, gun up, aiming at all of them one by one.

"How the hell are you still alive?" the colonel said, aiming his gun at him.

"It's a long story. Now drop your weapons, or the doc here gets it." He pointed the gun at Rachael, who was kneeling by Marissa.

"Don't do it. He will kill us all anyway," Rachael said, pleading with the colonel and the others as they threw their guns to the side and raised their hands in the air.

Again, the radio crackled to life. Again, it was Jackson on the other end, trying to get a response. "Does anyone copy? This is Private Jackson. We're on approach."

Rachael reached for her radio.

"Don't you fucking touch it," Brent said.

A few seconds later, they heard a huge explosion outside the complex.

"What the fuck was that?" Captain Miller said, glaring menacingly at Brent.

"I wouldn't threaten a man with a gun," Brent said, laughing. "Besides, I don't know. It wasn't me."

"Was that the plane my son was on?" Smith dropped to his knees, balling his hands into fists. "I'm going to kill you."

Smith got to his feet, and Brent hit him. Tears streamed down the sergeant's face. He shouldn't have left his son. That was all he could think. Whatever happened to Tom, it was all his fault.

"Listen, Brent, I know you hate all of us. But there is something bigger going on here. The general is going to release Compound Z overseas. If that happens, millions more will die," Rachael said, pleading.

Brent walked over to the general and pointed the gun in his face. "So, is it true?" Brent asked.

"Yes, it's true," General Rhodes said.

"Tell me how you were going to do this," Brent asked.

"My men were supposed to capture an infected person and take their blood and inject it into someone going on an outbound flight," General Rhodes explained.

"Was it done?" Brent asked, still pointing the gun in his face.

"I don't know. I was cut off. Before I hung up, they were starting to get overrun by infected at the airport," General Rhodes said.

"We need to know if they succeeded with the plan. Someone had to have survived after they dropped the cure," Rachael said, pleading with Brent.

"I guess you forgot about one thing?" Brent replied.

"And what is that?" Rachael asked, puzzled.

"I don't give a fuck," Brent replied.

"Well, Brent, my daughter Marissa there was supposed to kill Rachael and get the cure," the general said, getting up from his chair.

Brent watched him closely.

"You can take her place. I need a man who isn't scared of getting his hands dirty. As a show of good faith, here." General Rhodes slid a piece of paper to Brent.

"What's this?" Brent asked, looking at the piece of paper.

"That is where my new FOB is," General Rhodes replied.

"Let me think about it." As soon as he said the words, Brent pulled the trigger, blowing the general's brains out and sending him flying back over his chair. "My answer is no," Brent said, laughing.

The colonel jumped on top of Brent, grabbing the gun in an attempt to wrestle it from him. Sergeant Smith joined in the fray.

Captain Miller ran over to Rachael's side.

"Are you all right?" Rachael asked, kneeling to help Marissa.

"I don't think so," Marissa replied.

"Don't worry. We just need to stop the bleeding," Rachael said.

"No. I don't have much time. I'm sorry for everything. Ellen wasn't supposed to get killed. Brent came and fucked everything up. Here, take this." She handed over the cure to Rachael. "Don't let Jessica get it. Her plans are just as bad as the general's," Marissa said, coughing up blood.

"What was her plan?" Rachael asked.

But Marissa was gone. Rachael looked up at Captain Miller, tears falling down her face. "She didn't deserve this," Rachael said, tears freely flowing now.

Captain Miller looked up to see the men still struggling with Brent. Brent threw the colonel on the ground and punched the sergeant in the face, grabbing him with one hand and slamming him to the floor. The colonel jumped back on him, yelling, "Go with Captain Miller. I got this."

Just as Captain Miller was getting up to help, Marissa's body started to move. Rachael jumped back, and Captain Miller dragged her toward the door, followed by Sergeant Smith.

Brent threw the colonel to the ground again and looked at him. "Now you die," he said.

Marissa's body was now up and starting a full sprint at Brent. But she ran right passed him and hit Colonel Mailey at full speed, knocking him down and biting his neck. The colonel screamed. Brent grabbed his gun and shot in the direction of Captain Miller and the others, who were leaving the room.

As Captain Miller and Rachael ran down the hall, she glanced back and stopped. "Wait," she said.

The sergeant was leaning against the wall. They ran back to him. Blood seeped into his shirt and dripped from his lips. Rachael helped him slide to the floor and leaned him forward gently to examine the wound in his back. She looked up at Captain Miller, shaking her head, and helped him lie back against the floor.

"I know that look, Doc. It's not good, is it?" the sergeant said, now looking pale.

"Don't worry, man. If your son is alive, I will find him," Captain Miller said, tears starting to form as he watched his friend die.

"Captain, shoot him in the head right now," Rachael said.

"Why? He's already dead," Miller said angrily.

Just then, Smith's body jerked, and the captain quickly shot him. "You want to tell me what's going on?" Captain Miller said, the gun still smoking in his hand.

"I was wrong. Compound V isn't a cure. It just suppresses the infection until death. At that point, the Compound Z cells reactivate, but that doesn't explain why when Marissa was infected, she ran right past Brent," Rachael said, pacing back and forth in a tight loop.

"Wait. Is Brent infected?" Captain Miller asked, stopping her.

"When he and his brother started working with us, Jessica said she needed healthy people to try a new compound. I remember it was Compound X. His brother got sick right away and died, no other effects. But nothing happened to Brent, except he did get a little more violent. No other tests were done related to him. Brent could be infected with a different strand of Compound Z," Rachael mused.

"We have to go back and kill him if he's infected. He could spread it, right?" Captain Miller asked, looking at her.

Captain Miller and Rachael approached the glass door of the office and saw blood on the window. Captain Miller drew his gun from his side holster, trying to peer through the glass. As he slowly opened the door, Brent slammed into the door, knocking him backward. Opening the door, he grabbed Rachael and held the knife to her neck.

Captain Miller quickly popped up, gun still in hand, pointing it in Brent's direction. "Brent, let her go," Captain Miller said, pleading with Brent.

"Fuck you. This bitch dies here," Brent said, holding the knife closer to her throat.

"Brent, we need her and the cure formula," Captain Miller said, still pleading.

"I'm listening," Brent said.

"Listen, if the general's plan is true, she is the only one who can make more of the cure. You can't tell me you want to see all this happen again everywhere. We both lost a lot of people," Captain Miller said.

"Even if I believe you, I killed too many people to come back," Brent said.

"There is always a chance to come back and build trust," Captain Miller said, putting his gun in his holster and putting his hands up. "See, I put my gun away to show you that we can start to trust each other. Now put down the knife."

Brent released his grip on Rachael and lowered his knife. With a loud thud, his eyes rolled back into his head and he fell to the floor. Standing behind him was Corporal Hicks, holding a pipe in his hand.

"Are you both all right?" Hicks asked.

"Yes, thank you," Rachael replied.

"How the hell did you get here?" Captain Miller asked.

"It's a long story. I will explain on the way out of here," Hicks said.

"Hold on," Captain Miller said. Pulling his gun, he shot Brent five times in the chest and once in the head and turned. "Let's go," he said, walking down the hall.

Hicks walked past Brent lying on the floor, kicking him as he left. Then he turned and followed Captain Miller and Rachael out toward the main exit.

Chapter 13

Raven Squadron

The Raven Squadron was an elite squad that had been around for decades. The Ravens worked directly for the president and vice president. Chosen from the best of all military branches and hired in secret, the Ravens were always above the law. They were sent out to complete a task by the president or vice president and had no official ties to any government. Over the years, their power had been abused. Raven Squadron had been sent out to kill people of power, politicians who didn't align with the views of the president or vice president. Now, the man put in charge of Raven Squadron was the vice president's son, Tim Price.

Tim started out in the marines. He did two tours in Afghanistan with his unit. He got an honorable discharge only because of who his father was. Tim could beat a confession out of anyone. The marines always looked the other way, until he beat a woman. The woman was carrying bombs. Tim knew she was going to blow up some of his friends when they caught her. The interrogation kept going even after she'd told them everything. Tim just lost it. He was court-martialed, and his dishonorable discharge would have been the end of his career. But then his dad, the vice president, had him signed up for Raven Squadron. After that, it was all over. Tim worked his way up to captain as the Raven Squadron commander. In that capacity, he was able to use his skills with no consequences; no one could touch him now.

Tim and his men dropped from the helicopters just above the airport with full bio gear on and went inside.

There, an airport policeman approached them. "What's going on here? Are you here to get these people out? After the shit went down, a lot of people got stranded here," the cop said.

"Yes. We have our own pilots, and we need everyone to come here to the middle of the airport so we can test them. Then we will start boarding them and get you out of here. So, I need you to move fast," Tim said. "Move out," he yelled back to his men.

The cop turned and quickly made and announcementover the speaker, calling everyone to gather in the middle of the airport by proceeding toward the main gate as quickly and calmly as possible.

As Tim's men were setting up everything, the communications officer came over.

"Sir, I can't get the vice president or the facility on the radio. It might have been overrun or something else is wrong, sir," the officer said.

Tim called over a sergeant. "Sergeant, keep on mission. I want these people tested and on a plane out of here before I get back," Tim said.

"Yes, sir. But where are you going?" the sergeant replied.

"If the vice president is in trouble, he will need my help. Now *go*!" Tim yelled.

Tim and his squad of six men climbed into one of the helicopters on the roof and headed toward the facility. As they were flying over the area, Tim saw hundreds of people heading to the airport—both running on foot or driving, many erratically. Not too far behind them, he saw why—hundreds, maybe thousands of infected.

"Hand me that radio," Tim said. "Sergeant, do you read me?"

"Yes, sir," the sergeant replied.

"You need to get your men out of there. There are hundreds of people coming to the airport, followed by hundreds, maybe thousands of infected."

"Sir, what about these people?"

"Fuck them. Get out now, or you all will be dead," Tim replied.

"Sir, I can't just leave all these people," the sergeant said.

"Fine. It's your call. Over and out." Tim shut off the radio.

The sergeant called over all the twelve men who'd been left with him. "All right, men, we have a decision to make. We can all leave now, but we'll be leaving everyone here to die. Or we can stay and try to get everyone on the planes and get them out of here. I'm staying," he said.

Everyone looked around at each other, and all together they said they would stay to get these people out of here.

"All right. Officer, start getting all these people on the plane now," the sergeant said.

"We can't fit all these people on this plane," the officer said.

"You need to put as many people on as possible, or they're all going to die. Cram everyone in every available space now," the sergeant instructed urgently.

"Yes, sir," the officer replied, yelling at the remaining officers and staff to start moving.

"All right, they're coming. Take positions around the windows. Short, controlled bursts. And shoot at only what you can hit to save on ammo. There will be people running, along with infected. And we don't know who's infected, so just aim for everyone. We already know that everyone here isn't infected. If you hesitate, you will die," the sergeant said as everyone was taking up positions around the airport.

A car crashed through the barricade and headed for the airport's main building. A few seconds later, people on foot came running through the wrecked barricade, all heading for the airport.

"Take that car out. If it hits the building, we will be compromised," the sergeant yelled.

The men took aim, shooting at the car and taking out its tires. The car veered sideways and then flipped over and over.

Hundreds of people ran through the destroyed barricade, followed by the infected, who tackled them to the ground, biting and ripping them apart.

"Open fire," the sergeant yelled.

The men opened fire, hitting anything moving on the ground, not sure who was infected and who wasn't. People screamed and yelled, running everywhere. The men keep switching out mags. The sergeant knew at this rate and with so many targets, they were going to run out of ammo fast. He looked at the far wall to his left and saw the first of his men get jumped on by an infected.

"Fall back now," he yelled.

The men started to fall back a little at a time, as more and more infected made it to the windows. Another one of his men went down and then another.

"You two"—he pointed to the closest men—"come with me. Everyone else, fall back to the choppers. If we're not there in five, leave without us," the sergeant yelled.

"What are we doing, sir?" one of the soldiers asked, running with him.

"We're making sure the people are on the fucking plane," the sergeant replied.

As the men ran down the hall, they saw two police officers getting people on some planes.

"We need to move faster. We're getting overrun," the sergeant yelled at the officers.

"This plane's almost full. We're going as fast as possible," one the police officer's said, worried and sweating.

Just then, the glass shattered behind them. The infected poured down one of the ramps, and the soldiers and police officers opened fire, taking out as many as they could.

"You two, get these officers on the plane and you go with them. I'll go down to the next sections to see if there's anyone left," the sergeant said to his men, still shooting.

As he ran down the other ramp, he turned to see one of his men taken down from behind by an infected. The other managed to close the door to the plane just in time.

As the sergeant got to the other sections of the airport, he saw a man standing by the door. "What the fuck are you doing?" he asked.

"Waiting. There was a guy who ran into the restroom after his son," the man replied.

The sergeant ran into the bathroom to get the man and his kid. When he came out, he saw the first man holding the door and fighting off two infected. The sergeant ran into one of them, throwing it aside. When he turned to fight the second one, it bit his hand. He pulled his sidearm out and shot both the infected in the head.

"Go. Shut the door. Get on the plane now," the sergeant yelled to the two men and the kid.

"What about you?" the man said.

"I'll be fine. Go," the sergeant replied.

The man slammed the door shut. The sergeant aimed his sidearm and killed two more infected near him and then put the gun to his own head.

The sign above the sergeant read, "Flight 1720 Paris."

One of the men in the chopper with Tim leaned over and spoke. "We just got confirmation, sir. Four of the twelve men we left got out on choppers, sir. What do you want them to do?"

"Tell them to head back to base and wait for us there," Tim replied.

As Tim and his team were on their way to the facility, the pilot spotted a plane in the air dropping what looked like gas. "Sir, you might want to see this," the pilot said.

Tim went to the front of the chopper, looked out the window, and saw the plane dropping what looked like gas bombs. "What the hell are they dropping?" he asked.

"Not sure, sir. But it looks like whatever they're dropping is killing the infected," the copilot said, looking through his binoculars.

Tim looked through the binoculars. He watched the infected stop moving and drop dead as the gas fell. "Raise that aircraft now," he instructed.

The pilot hailed the aircraft. "This is Raven One to aircraft dropping the gas, do you hear? I repeat, this is Raven One."

"This is Corporal Hicks. We read you," Hicks said.

"This is Captain Tim Price with Raven Squadron. Are you Corporal Hicks with General Rhodes?" Tim asked.

"Yes, sir," Hicks replied.

"What are you dropping, Corporal?" Tim asked.

"It's called Compound V, sir. It kills infected and inoculates anyone who's infected that hasn't turned yet, sir," Hicks replied.

"Did you make that at the facility?" Tim asked.

"Yes, sir. A scientist named Rachael came up with it," Hicks replied.

"Finish your run and drop some of that gas by the airport about twenty miles from here. There are a lot of infected there. And when you're done, return to the Raven's Nest," Tim said.

"Yes, sir. Understood," Hicks said.

"What the hell is Raven's Nest?" Jackson asked Hicks.

Hicks just shrugged.

"Let's finish our drop and hit that airport he was talking about and get back to the facility," Hayes said.

Hayes tapped Hicks on the shoulder and gestured for him to come to the back with him. They both walked to the back of the plane, and Hayes raised his sidearm to Hicks.

"I know you know what Raven's Nest is," Hayes said.

"What do you mean?" Hicks said.

"I saw how you acted when he said it," Hayes said.

"It means get rid of your expendable cargo. That means you and Jackson," Hicks said.

"You motherfucker," Hayes said, putting the gun even closer to Hicks's face.

Just then, Tom came to the back. He yelled when he saw the gun, drawing Hayes's attention briefly. This gave Hicks just enough time to grab the gun and land a punch to Hayes's face, sending him toppling backward on the plane's floor.

Hicks pointed the gun at Hayes. "It's not personal. It's just business," he said and shot Hayes in the head.

The kid tried to run toward the cockpit, but Hicks grabbed him and slammed him to the floor, knocking him out. Hicks headed to the cockpit.

"What the hell was that? Sounded like a gunshot back there." Jackson glanced back at Hicks to see a gun in his face.

"Sorry, Jackson. Orders are orders," Hicks said.

"So, the Raven's Nest was for you?" Jackson said.

"That's right," Hicks replied.

"You killed Hayes and Smith's kid. You piece of shit," Jackson cried.

"Kid's going down with the ship," Hicks said.

Jackson dove for the gun, and Hicks put two rounds in his chest, flinging him back into his seat, where he sat looking up at Hicks, bleeding out.

"Just so you know, I've always liked you. It's just orders," Hicks said. He took the plane off autopilot; put one round into Jackson's head, killing him; and grabbed a parachute off the wall.

Tom woke up. He looked at Hicks with frightened eyes.

"Here," Hicks said, throwing Tom the other parachute.

"I don't know what to do," Tom said, crying.

"Put it on. Jump. And pull the string. After that, you're on your own, kid," Hicks said, jumping out and aiming himself toward the facility.

Tom looked out the plane door and started to cry. "I want my daddy," he said.

Then he wiped his eyes and jumped.

Chapter 14

Brent's Rampage

Captain Miller, Rachael, and Hicks reached the front door to the facility and saw some army guys standing in the main lobby, guns drawn and pointed at them.

"Who are you?" Captain Miller said, his gun pointed back at the soldiers.

"We're the Raven Squadron. Who are you?" Tim asked.

"I'm Captain Miller. What are you doing here?"

"We're here to pick up Dr. Morgan and her formula. And this is her, I presume," Tim said, pointing at Rachael.

"I don't think so. She is staying with me," Captain Miller said, pointing his gun right at Tim.

As they stood there, looking at each other, guns drawn, Captain Miller felt a gun to the back of the head.

"Sorry, Captain. But we are taking the doc," Hicks said.

"What the hell are you doing?" Rachael said.

"I'm Raven Squadron, and I had my own mission here. So, I'm sorry, but we need that formula. Now hand it over—now," Hicks said.

Rachael slowly put her hand in her pocket and felt that the formula was gone. Thinking back over all that had happened, she remembered that Brent had grabbed her from behind. "I don't have it. Brent does. He must have taken it when he grabbed me," she said.

"Where is this Brent?" Tim asked.

"He's dead in the back hallway. The captain here shot him," Hicks said.

"Where is the vice president?" Tim asked.

"Last I heard, Brent shot him. Haven't seen him since," the captain said.

Tim paced back and forth. Then he slammed the butt of his gun on the desk, breaking it. "You two, go and search Brent's body for the formula and look for my father! Now," he screamed.

Brent was waking up slowly. Looking down at his hand, he saw the drive with the cure on it and remembered that someone had hit him in the back. Looking down, he saw the black ooze again, this time coming from his chest. Reaching up, he felt his head and found ooze there too. "That fucker shot me in the head," he said.

Hearing footsteps, he pulled his knife from his belt and lay back down. He heard two soldiers talking. When they stopped and leaned over him, he jumped up, slicing open the stomach of one of the soldiers. The other, startled, tried for his gun. Brent turned just before he could get his gun free. Grabbing the soldier's arms, with one quick blow, he headbutted him, knocking him out. The first soldier, clutching his stomach with one hand, reached for his gun with the other. Just as he freed it from its holster, Brent threw the knife, sticking it into his eye and killing him instantly.

Brent dragged the unconscious soldier to the nearby security office, where he found some scalpels. He bound the soldiers arms and legs and threw some water on him to wake him up.

"Who the fuck are you?" Brent asked.

"Fuck you," the soldier said, spitting at Brent.

"Have you ever seen what a scalpel does to skin? It cuts like butter," Brent said. He cut into his shoulder, and the soldier screamed. Brent grabbed another scalpel and started on his other shoulder without asking another question.

"I'm Bill with Raven Squadron," Bill yelled as pain drilled through his shoulder.

"Bill, what is your squadron doing here?" Brent asked.

Bill didn't say anything. He just stared at Brent.

Brent took another scapula and stabbed it into his other shoulder.

Bill yelled out in pain. "We were sent here to meet the general and the vice president and get the cure from a doctor and complete Operation Raven's Nest," Bill said between gasps of pain.

"What's Operation Raven's Nest?" Brent asked.

"We were supposed to infect some people on various planes and send them out. But we lost communication with this facility, so the captain came to see what was going on," Bill said, adding, "We also were supposed to kill everyone at this facility."

"Thanks for the information," Brent said, putting another scalpel into Bill's leg.

"I told you everything," Bill said, screaming out in pain.

"I never told you I was going to stop, did I?" Brent said, cutting into his other leg.

Bill yelled out again.

"What the fuck is taking those idiots so long? You go see what's taking them so long," Tim said, pointing to one of his men.

"Yes, sir," the marine replied.

A few minutes later, his voice came over the radio. "Captain, Ted is dead, has a knife through his eye. And Bill is missing. Looks like his body was dragged upstairs," the marine said.

"Hicks, I thought you said he was dead. Take Doug and get Jeff. Find and kill this motherfucker. I want his head on a fucking stick," Tim yelled.

Captain Miller and Rachael traded glances.

Hicks and Doug came around the corner and met Jeff. They saw him still looking at Ted's body.

"Look at this shit, man. Who the fuck is this guy?" Jeff said, pointing to the knife in Ted's eye.

"Who fucking cares? Let's just go kill this guy," Doug said.

"Who cares? Both guys were fucking marines, some of the best," Jeff said with some worry in his voice.

"Don't underestimate this guy. He's fucking crazy," Hicks said.

"We'll see just how dangerous this guy is," Doug said. Pushing his way past Hicks and Jeff, he headed toward the drag marks, Jeff and Hicks following.

Doug, Jeff, and Hicks went up the stairs, guns drawn. Once they'd rounded the corners, Hicks made a hand gesture, signaling to open the door the trail they were following disappeared behind.

Jeff opened the door. Doug went in first, followed by Hicks.

Inside, they saw Bill strapped to a chair with scalpels sticking out of him everywhere. Doug slowly approached him. As he got closer, he saw that the scalpels weren't just in his arms and legs but in his chest and jaw. There was even one in one eye.

"Be careful," Hicks whispered.

"Careful of what? He's dead," Doug said, not being quiet.

Doug examined Bill's body. Looking at his stomach, he saw a blinking red light and pulled his shirt back. There, a glass jar filled with scalpels was hooked to what he suddenly realized was a makeshift explosive device.

"Everyone get—"

Before all the words could leave Doug's mouth, the glass jar exploded, knocking both Jeff and Hicks back against the wall.

As Hicks tried to get up, he blinked his eyes, struggling to focus. In a haze, he saw Doug's legs just standing there alone, their torso gone, and nothing left of Bill's body in the chair.

He looked at Jeff. Scalpels had embedded in his face and arms and legs. Jeff, was had been standing in front of him, had taken most of the blast's impact. Hicks examined himself and saw he had a scalpel in his left arm. Hicks's vision was still a little blurry, but he saw someone enter the room. Before Hicks could raise his gun, the man grabbed the gun away from Hicks. Hicks heard Brent's voice.

"I bet you thought that was funny hitting me in the back of the fucking head. You should have killed me." Brent chuckled and knocked Hicks out with the butt of the rifle.

When Hicks woke up again, his head hurt just as much as before. He tried to move his hands, only to find they were tied behind his back, and then he remembered hearing Brent's voice.

"Welcome back, Sleeping Beauty. You're just in time," Brent said.

"In time for what?" Hicks replied.

"You're going with me. I'm going to trade you for the doc," Brent said.

"Tim will never trade me for the doctor," Hicks replied.

"I don't expect him to, but he will trade for this," Brent said, holding up the data card that had the cure on it.

"Then why are you bringing me? Why don't you just kill me?"

"What's the fun in that? I need a meat shield if it goes south," Brent said, laughing as he pushed Hicks in front of him down the hall.

Brent made his way into the main hall with his rifle swung over Hick's right shoulder, using him as a shield. As he stepped into the main hall, he saw Captain Miller sitting in a chair on the far right side and Dr. Morgan sitting on the floor next to Captain Tim Price and three more Raven Squadron members. Captain Robertson was the first to see Brent and Hicks, and he drew his rifle and aimed in their direction. His three men quickly followed suit.

Chapter 15

Tim vs. Dave

"Stop right there, motherfucker," Tim said.

"I'm here to trade for the doc," Brent said.

"Trade for what? I'll kill you and Hicks right now," Tim yelled back.

"Not for this sack of shit. For this," Brent said, holding up the cure data card in his left hand. He quickly put the card away.

"What if I have Scott here shoot you both and take it?" Tim said.

Scott raised his rifle, but before he could get it to his shoulder, he dropped to the floor, blood oozing from a round fired into his head by Brent.

"Two reasons. First I have the drop on you. And I could kill you and just take the bitch. And second of all, if there's a chance you do kill me before I kill you, I will drop this little grenade"—he flashed an object in his left hand—"killing Hicks and destroying the data card. Believe me when I say I will kill the doc before I die, and you will have nothing." Brent snarled.

"Fine. I'll send the doc over. You toss me the data card," Tim said.

"Sir, he just killed Scott. We're not letting this asshole out of here," one of the other soldiers said.

"We're about to get the data card. So shut the fuck up," Tim said.

"Wait, sir. Where are Doug and Jeff?" the other soldier asked.

"Where are my other men?" Tim yelled to Brent.

"They're dead. Are we making the switch or what?"

With a groan, Tim grabbed Rachael and told her to walk slowly toward Brent.

Just as she started to walk, a voice came from the other side of the room. "I'm afraid I can't let you do that." The voice belonged to a man wearing the insignia of a captain. Two other men and one woman in military fatigues stood behind him, rifles aimed strategically at all of them.

"Who the fuck are you?" Tim yelled, gun at his side.

"Captain Dave Craven, Raven Squadron," Craven replied.

"You can't be. We are Raven Squadron," Tim said.

"You were. Now we are. Your team has been disbanded. Now, hand over the doctor. Or you will all be killed," Craven said.

Tim took a second to think about this new information before he answered.

"Sergeant Hill," Craven said.

She fired a shot right by his ear, just grazing it.

"All right, all right. She is coming your way," Tim yelled back, grabbing his ear and letting the doctor go.

Rachael changed directions, now walking toward Captain Craven. Seeing this, Brent turned Hicks with the gun resting on Hicks's shoulder. "She is fucking mine," he yelled and opened fire.

Faster than even Brent thought possible, Captain Craven grabbed Rachael and pulled her over the nearest desk as shots from Brent's gun sprayed across it. Sergeant Hill and the others ducked behind other desks.

Frank, one of the other marines with Tim, saw an open shot on Brent. Remembering what Brent had done to Scott and his other friend, Frank took aim. Just as he pressed the trigger, Tim bumped him, making the shot go wide. The bullet only grazed Brent's left arm.

Brent stopped shooting at Captain Craven and his marines and looked at Frank just standing there. "You motherfucker," he yelled, unloading shot after shot into Frank until his gun clicked.

Remembering the grenade in his left hand, he threw it in the direction of Tim and Frank and shoved Hicks in the direction of Captain Craven and ran down the hall in the other direction.

Tim saw the grenade land near him and pushed Frank on top of the grenade just as it went off, blowing Frank's dead body in half and splattering blood everywhere.

Sergeant Hill popped up from her spot and unloaded her rifle on Hicks, dropping him. All this happened almost simultaneously.

"Clear," Hill yelled.

Everyone got up from behind the desks. Captain Craven walked over to where Tim was hiding and saw his men dead.

"You're a piece of shit, killing your own man like that," Captain Craven said, looking down at the mess.

"It was either him or both of us. The math was easy," Tim retorted.

"Hill, take the doc to the helicopter. If anyone comes out other than the three of us, kill them," Captain Craven ordered.

"Yes, sir," Hill replied.

"Tim, where is the cure data card?" Captain Craven asked.

"The guy who everyone here calls Brent, the one who just ran down the hall there, has it," Tim replied.

"Where is the vice president?" Captain Craven asked.

"Brent killed my father. That's what Captain Miller said," Tim replied.

"Saves us the trouble. Jacobs, find and kill Captain Miller. Dallas, find this Brent. Get the data card. Bring it to me. You both have ten minutes. Then we leave. You can follow in one of the other choppers since Jacobs can fly," Captain Craven ordered.

"What about that piece of shit?" Jacobs said, pointing to Tim.

"He's mine. Now move," Captain Craven barked.

"Yes, sir," Jacobs and Dallas replied in unison before taking off in opposite directions.

Dave turned back to Tim. "Lose the gun," he said.

Tim threw his gun down the hall. "Now, I'm sure they gave the order Raven's Nest," he said.

"Yes," Dave said, pulling his knife from his belt and throwing his gun down.

"So, it's like that," Tim said, pulling his knife from his belt.

"Not that you deserve it, but I want to see just how good you are. You kill me, you walk," Dave replied.

"Just so you know, after I kill you, I'm killing everyone in your squadron," Tim said.

Tim swiped with his knife; Dave jumped back. Tim tried again; Dave again jumped back. Tim stabbed with his knife. Dave caught his hand, and Tim grabbed Dave's hand, and they were stuck struggling. Tim headbutted Dave, sending him back over to the nearest desk. Tim jumped over the desk and tried to jump on top of Dave.

Dave got his feet between himself and Tim, kicking him back over the desk and jumping back to his feet. When Tim tried to stab Dave again, this time, Dave spun out of the way, driving his knife into Tim's left shoulder and then ducking as Tim tried to swipe at Dave's head. As Dave ducked, he sliced Tim's stomach, and Tim stumbled backward.

Tim charged Dave with a downward stab. Dave caught Tim's arm and then drove his knife into his arm, simultaneously breaking his hand. Tim dropped the knife. Dave kicked the back of Tim's knees, bringing him to the floor and brought his knife to Tim's throat.

"I thought you were good," Dave said, holding the knife to Tim's throat.

"Fuck you," Tim replied, spiting at Dave.

"Any last words, you piece of shit?" Dave said.

"No. But your guy Dallas is dead. You shouldn't have sent him after that Brent guy," Tim said, laughing.

"Who's Brent? Dallas is a marine," Dave replied.

"Won't matter. Brent has already killed five of my marines," Tim said, laughing again.

Dave slit Tim's throat and kicked him to the ground and then grabbed his walkie. "Dallas, come in, you hear me," Dave said with a little worry in his voice. Looking at his watch, he noted that both men had only five minutes left to get back to the chopper.

"Jacobs, you read me?" Dave said over the walkie.

"Yes, sir. I'm tracking Miller, sir. Over," Jacobs replied.

"I can't get a hold of Dallas. Have you seen him?" Dave asked.

"He followed that other guy into the science wing. I'm sure there's a lot of equipment in there. It's probably messing with the signal," Jacobs said.

"Find Miller and check on Dallas if he doesn't come back. I have a bad feeling about this. I'm going to the chopper. You have four minutes," Dave said.

"Yes, sir. Over and out," Jacobs said, signing off.

Back at the landing pad, Dave climbed into the chopper and gave the pilot the signal to lift off.

"You think Jacobs will actually kill Miller?" Hill asked.

"Why wouldn't he?" Dave replied.

"I recognized him. He was Jacobs's captain for a while before he took the special ops stuff for the marines and Jacobs got transferred to you," Hill said.

"He had better, or Jacobs will have to be eliminated under Raven's Nest protocol," Dave replied as they chopper left.

Chapter 16

Truth

Jacobs found Captain Miller going through Jessica's desk looking for something. He came up with a set of keys and turned around to see Jacobs standing there, rifle pointing at him.

"You going to kill me?"

Jacobs lowered his gun. "No. I know you, sir. You were my captain before I was under Captain Craven's command," Jacobs said.

"Where did they take Dr. Morgan?" Captain Miller asked.

"They took her to see the president. The location is a black site, not on the books, so I'm told. Captain Craven says it's where presidents go when they want to take care of business that's not on the books. It's not just because of our history that I don't want to kill you, Captain Miller, sir. I need your help stopping the president and some doctor named Price," Jacobs said.

"Dr. Jessica Price. What is she doing with the president? I thought the vice president was the one behind all this. Isn't he still alive?" Captain Miller asked.

"Maybe he is. I don't know anything about that. The last time we saw the president, he ordered the army to start dropping napalm on the entire quarantine area. That Jessica doctor said there was no stopping the infection. As far as the vice president, he was infected. So Jessica said she had to put him down."

"What? We dropped the cure. It works," Miller said.

"Even if he knows that, he's killing them all," Jacobs said.

"Well then, let's get going. I have Jessica's keys to her private chopper," Captain Miller said.

"First, we need to find my friend Dallas. He went after the other guy," Jacobs said.

"Brent? He should be dead. I shot him in the chest and head. I guess he'd infected. And if your guy went after him by himself, he might be dead," Captain Miller said.

"Dead? What are you talking about?" Jacobs said, looking concerned.

"Brent's dangerous. Somehow, from what Rachael said, the infection bonded with him. It made him stronger, faster. And apparently, he can heal somehow. Everyone who's gone after him one-on-one is dead. Grab you gun. Let's see if we can find him before Brent does," Captain Miller said, grabbing his own gun.

"Hope we do," Jacobs said.

"We need to find Brent anyway. He has the cure data card," Miller said, adding, "I know you said you served under me. But don't take it personal if I don't entirely trust you yet."

Miller started up the stairs, followed by Jacobs. As they made their way down the hall, they saw blood seeping from underneath a closed door. Miller pointed and gestured for Jacobs to get into position and then pull the door open. As Jacobs swung open the door, Miller rushed in. Blood was splattered around the room, and scalpels had been embedded into the drywall everywhere.

Jacobs came in next. Seeing some men on the ground, he checked the bodies. "None of these guys are Dallas," he said.

"What about one of these guys?" Miller said, pointing to two pairs of legs, one pair tied to a chair and the other pair slumped on the ground in front of the chair. All that remained of the owners of those legs were piles of blood and guts strewn about.

"I don't think so. It looks like they were both killed by an explosion. Let's keep moving," Jacobs said, swallowing down the bile working its way up the back of his throat.

As they moved down the hall, Brent jumped out from the room at the end of the hallway and opened fire, spraying bullets down the hall. Jacobs and Miller dove to the floor, and Miller returned fire as Brent ran down the stairs toward the exit. Jacobs jumped up and ran down the hall, swinging open the door to the room Brent had come out of. He saw Dallas pinned to the wall by knives, barely alive.

Before Jacobs could enter, Miller grabbed his arm. "Hold on," he said.

"Hold on? He's dying," Jacobs yelled.

"Brent wants us to go rescue him. It's what he does," Miller said.

Miller left, rushing back with an office chair from another room and rolled it into the room, shutting the door behind it. A few seconds later, they heard an explosion.

Miller slowly opened the door, seeing the chair had been destroyed. "I think we're good," he said.

Jacobs went in and pulled out the knives pinning his friend to the wall and then gently helped him down.

"Sorry, sir. I told him everything," Dallas said, coughing up blood.

"Don't worry about it. We will kill that son of a bitch for you," Jacobs said as Dallas died. Jacobs slammed his fists on the floor.

Jacobs sets Dallas on the floor. Getting to his feet, he looked at Miller. "We need to go kill that fucking guy."

"Get in line. He killed a lot of our friends," Miller said, head hanging down. He put his hand on Jacob's shoulder.

"We know he's going for the president. After he kills him, we kill that guy," Jacobs yelled.

"I don't think he's going to kill the president; I think he's going to trade the data card for Dr. Morgan. We need to get there and make sure he doesn't kill her," Miller said.

"What makes this doctor everybody wants so goddamn important?" Jacobs yelled.

"She's the only one who knows how to make the cure. If she dies and something happens to the card, we're fucked. We need to go now," Miller said.

As they got into the secret chopper and Miller started it up, he asked, "Do you think your team will help us stop both the president and Brent?"

"Not the captain. He's one those we-don't-ask-why, we-do-and-die guys. Hill, I think she will. After she hears that Brent killed Dallas, she'll kill him herself. He was like a brother to her," Jacobs said.

Miller took the helicopter off the landing pad, and they started toward the secret base according to Jacobs's directions.

Captain Craven and Sergeant Hill marched Rachael Morgan into a room and shoved her to the floor in front of a couch. She looked to see the biggest man she had ever seen.

"I see you have met, Felix. Please, Felix, help Dr. Morgan to her feet and into the chair," the president said as he walked into the room.

Felix grabbed Rachael with little effort and threw her into the chair harder than he'd intended.

"Thanks." Rachael scowled, rubbing her arm.

"Sorry. Felix doesn't always know his own strength. Captain Craven, you and Sergeant Hill can wait outside the door please," the president said.

"What the hell do you want?" Rachael said angrily.

"I want to know more about Compound Z."

"I don't know what you're talking about," Rachael replied.

"Please don't insult my intelligence. My men raided your research facility, so don't lie to me again." This time, the president's voice carried a hint of anger.

Just then, Jessica entered through the same door the president had come in, smiling at her. "Go ahead and tell him what you think it is," Jessica said, sitting down right next to the president.

"Compound Z is something that has limitless medical capabilities. It can cure cancer and heal people with the most devastating injuries you can imagine. It's derived from the original Compound, X," Rachael said.

"But you're forgetting one thing—the side effects. It turns people into zombie-like creatures. I would say that's a big drawback," the president said.

"Yes, but with the cure, now we can perhaps tame it. Besides, Compound X wasn't completely bad. Brent survived and is fine—no side effects. But it did kill his brother. With a little more time, it could become the whole cure. Isn't that right Rachael?" Jessica said, staring at her.

"I was working on fixing it. I needed more time. But Brent is infected. I don't know how, but he is. The side effects are you become psychotic.

Brent was never like this. Now he just wants me dead for killing his brother."

"So, you released this compound in a small town to see what would happen?" the president prompted.

"That wasn't me. I told General Rhodes and Jessica it needed more work. She didn't care," Rachael said, angered.

"That was a military decision. We were working at a military facility. I had no authority. You were the doctor there. You should have stepped up," Jessica replied, looking at the president.

"So, you let Rhodes release this compound, and now millions of people have died," the president said angrily.

"You're one to talk," Rachael said, pointing at the screens, which displayed scenes in which soldiers were killing people, shooting them down and pulling them out of their cars and planes dropping bombs.

"That is cleaning up your mess." The president stood up. Walking around, he looked at the screens. "None of these people had to die. Their blood is on your hands, not mine."

"I created a cure for this. We dropped it to kill the infected and cure those who were infected but hadn't turned yet," Rachael replied, almost yelling.

Felix stood in front of her, making her shrink into her seat.

"What is Compound V then?" the president asked.

"That's the cure," she replied.

"But it's not, is it? It contains the virus," Jessica said, looking at the screens with the president.

"How did you find that out? I only just found it out," Rachael said.

"I know that because Jessica here told me you were arming a plane to drop it on everyone to help them. And secondly, right after we heard about a cure, we started rounding everyone up to see if this cure worked. We had a man have a heart attack. Doctors brought him to the emergency room here, where they tried to help him. When he died, minutes later, he jumped up, attacking the people who had tried to save him. We lost twenty-seven people over all before we were able to put down all the infected," the president explained.

"I can fix it. I just need my lab and an infected person, preferably one who has already transformed," Rachael said, pleading.

"I'm sorry. Your facility has been destroyed. And as for finding an infected, we will kill any infected with Compound Z or V," the president said.

"I can't believe you did that. Compound Z can help everyone," Rachael said angrily. She started to stand up, but Felix shoved her back into the chair.

"That Compound Z is just too dangerous. It may seem like it can help, but it will destroy us all if we let it. That's why it has to be wiped off the face of the earth and never be let out again," the president said.

As the president and Rachael were arguing, Felix held his ear. After listening to something that came over his earpiece, he walked over to the president and whispered into his ear. The president shook his head, and Felix said something into a microphone that Rachael couldn't hear. The president went back to the couch and took a sip of a drink he'd poured. Setting the glass on the table, he looked right at Rachael.

"I want to know more about Brent. What can you tell me?" he asked.

Rachael was ready to go another round over Compound Z. And this question caught her off guard. Her face turned shocked and scared. *Is he here?* she thought to herself.

"Dr. Morgan, please tell me who Brent is again," the president said, shaking her out of her thoughts.

"As I said, he was injected with Compound X, and he is infected. And he is dangerous. Why do you ask?"

"If he's infected, how is he still alive?" Jessica asked. "I thought everyone who was infected died."

"It somehow bonded with him. Why does this even matter?" Rachael said.

"Because he is saying he will trade a data card with the cure on it," the president said.

Brent, after firing shots at Jacobs and Miller, ran out to the helicopter pad, where one chopper remained. It belonged to Tim, the vice president's son. As he climbed into the chopper, he looked at the pilot, who was still there, just on his phone. The pilot looked back, hearing someone get into the chopper.

"We ready to g—" The pilot stopped midsentence, as there was a gun pointing at his face.

"Go to these coordinates. And hurry. I have a date." Brent giggled to himself.

The pilot just looked at the paper Brent had given him and started the chopper. He knew a crazy person when he saw one, and he didn't want to get on this one's bad side. The pilot knew exactly where he was going. He also knew there wouldn't be a problem landing. With the Ravens Squadron logo on the side, no one would stop them or ask questions until they'd landed.

Hopefully, the people on the ground can deal with this psycho, he thought to himself.

As the pilot landed at the base where Brent's coordinates had led them, two men walked up to the chopper.

"Welcome back, sir," the guard on the right said as he opened the door to the chopper.

As he did, Brent's knife sailed through the air, hitting the guard who had been opening the chopper door in the head and killing him instantly.

The other guard went for his gun, but Brent was far faster and grabbed his hand before he could pull it from his holster.

"You're not Tim," the guard said, hand locked in Brent's grip.

"I know," Brent replied. And with a smooth motion, he cut the guard's throat.

Brent watched as the guard grabbed at his throat, blood squirting through his fingers. He stood like that for a moment before topping to the floor, gargling his own blood.

Brent turned back to the chopper to see that the pilot had taken off, leaving Brent there. Brent headed for the biggest building on the base. As he approached the building, two guards stood outside on guard. Brent walked up as if he was on a Sunday stroll and, flashing a smile, calmly asked the first guard, "Is the president in there?"

Both guards looked at each other and then at Brent.

The taller, more muscular looked right at Brent, leaning down a little down to, hopefully, intimidate Brent. "Yeah. And who the fuck are you?"

Brent, who'd been holding his knife behind his back, brought the weapon out with a swift whoosh and plunged it into the guard's neck.

Without pausing, he grabbed the shorter guard by his throat, breaking his neck; unclipped his security card; and opened the door the pair had been guarding.

As Brent walked down the hall, two guards saw him and drew their guns. "How the fuck did you get in here?" one of them asked.

"Need to see the president. I think I have something he wants." Brent waved the data card in the air.

Just then, Captain Craven and Hill come around the corner and saw Brent and the data card. Captain Craven got on his walkie to radio Felix in the room with the president.

"Please bring him in," the president said, pushing a button on his desk.

Captain Craven and Sergeant Hill, along with two agents, escorted Brent into the room. Brent looked around, smiling.

"My men tell me you have something for me," the president said, standing up.

"Well, that depends. Do you have something for me?" Brent said, looking right at Rachael.

"You can't trust him. He will kill everyone in this room. He has killed so many people already," Rachael said, pleading.

"Why shouldn't I have Felix shoot you and I'll just take the card? First, though, Dr. Morgan says you're infected. But you don't look infected. So, please tell me if she is telling me the truth." The president watched Brent closely as he said this.

"I'm not infected. She's crazy. If I was infected, I would have signs, and I don't. She wants me dead because her experiment with my brother and me didn't work. He died, and she wants me dead to cover it up," Brent said.

"That's a lie. I watched Captain Miller put four rounds into your chest and one in your head. Tell us how you're still alive," Rachael said, thinking she'd said too much when she saw Jessica look right at her, her eyes wide.

"If that was true, how would I be standing here? She's mistaken," Brent said, looking at Rachael.

"Well, you say she is lying. She says you are lying. I guess there's only one way to solve this," Jessica said, walking over to Felix. Grabbing his gun, she turned around, holding the gun behind her back.

"And how's that?" Brent said.

The moment he spoke, she took the gun from behind her back and shot Brent in the chest, knocking him against the wall and then to the floor.

"What the hell was that?" the president said, getting out of his chair.

"Think of it this way. It was a loose end, and now it's been tied off," Jessica said, walking over to his body and kneeling next to him. Grabbing the card, she stopped to look at the hole in Brent's chest leaking ooze. "Guess he was infected," she said. Looking back at the president, she stood up and aimed the gun at his head.

Before Jessica could pull the trigger, Captain Miller and Jacobs burst into the room, guns drawn.

"Let Rachael go now," Captain Miller said.

"Soldier, how did you get in here?" the president said.

"Most of your staff is dead—taken out by Brent over there. We walked right in. Now let her go," Captain Miller said.

"You don't know what's going on here," the president said.

"If you don't let her go, we will open fire," Captain Miller said.

"Jacobs, what the hell are you doing?" Captain Craven said.

"Sir, I can't sit by and watch all these people die at the border and let him get away with it. Dr. Morgan is the only one who can stop it," Jacobs replied.

"None of you understand what's going on here. Put down your weapons, and we can talk. If you don't, Felix will snap her neck," the president said.

"Listen, you can't trust Brent. He's gone crazy. Fine, we will put down our weapons. Just don't kill her." Captain Miller and Jacobs put down their weapons.

"Felix, put Rachael back in the chair." The president walked back to his desk and sat down.

Captain Miller looked down and saw Brent lying on the ground. "Who shot him?"

"Brent is out of play, so let's talk," the president said.

"No, he's not," Miller replied. "I shot him five times, and he survived. We all need to make a choice right now. Hill, Craven, you're either with us or against us here. The president is killing innocent people, and Brent killed our friends. So make a decision," Captain Miller said.

"Wait, these people are infected. They can still spread the virus," the president said.

"No. We dropped the cure. It's over," Captain Miller said.

"Tell him," the president said to Rachael.

"The cure works if they're alive. After death, the virus takes over, and they can become infected again. But I can fix it. I just need a little more time. I can make it work," Rachael said, pleading.

"I know, Rachael. I saw it firsthand with Marissa. She was still infected in the facility, and she was given the cure. If Rachael says she can fix it, we need to give her time," Captain Miller said, his hand on his gun.

Two agents who brought Brent to the office stepped behind the captain and Jacobs, hands on their guns.

"Hill, Brent killed Dallas," Jacobs said.

Hill pulled her gun and pointed it at Felix and Jessica.

"Hill, stand down," Captain Craven said.

"No, sir. We need to make a choice, sir, and I made mine," Hill said.

Brent popped to his feet, grabbed a knife he had hidden around his ankle, and plunged it into the eye of the agent standing right behind Captain Miller. Then he threw it at the president, striking him in the arm. The other agent jumped on Brent.

Captain Craven ran over to the president and helped him up, pulling the knife out of his arm.

"Get me out of here," the president yelled.

Captain Craven helped the president up and guided him toward the back door. As he did so, the president yelled to Felix, "*No one follows. Kill them all.*" and with that, Craven and the president slipped out the door.

Felix went for Rachael's throat. Captain Miller slammed into Felix, only managing to knock him back a few steps. Then Captain Miller threw a punch, and Felix caught it in his right hand. He pulled Miller forward, clotheslining him and sending him sprawling to the ground.

"Get Rachael," Captain Miller said, looking up at Jacobs. Then he sprang to his feet and jumped over the chair, landing a kick to Felix's chest that barely moved the giant.

Jacobs grabbed Rachael and brought her to the corner. "Stay here," he said.

Looking back, he saw Captain Miller fly over the chair where Rachael had been and land a huge uppercut to Felix's face. Seeing one of the guns on the ground, he went for it. But before he reached it, Felix grabbed his arm and threw him back against the wall. Felix started to punch Jacob's ribs; Jacobs heard and felt a crack in his ribs as the assault continued. Just as he thought it wouldn't end, Felix was gone. Jacobs went down on one knee, holding his ribs. He looked up to see Miller on Felix's back choking him. Scanning the room, he saw that Hill was on her own struggling with Brent across the room. He grabbed a wooden chair and raced across the room, bringing it down on Brent's head and knocking him out cold.

"Thanks," Hill said, gasping for air.

"No problem. Let's go help Miller. Then we will deal with Brent," Jacobs said. Turning around, he saw Miller, still clinging to Felix's back, was getting slammed against the wall.

Felix slammed Miller one last time, making him lose his grip. Felix turned and grabbed Miller by the throat, picking him off the ground with one arm and choking him. Jacob grabbed his knife from his belt and jammed it into Felix's shoulder, making him drop Miller. Felix spun around, grabbing Jacobs by his throat. Slamming him through the wooden table below, he pulled the knife from his shoulder and put it right through Jacob's leg.

Before Felix got up, Hill kneed him in the face and knocked him back. Then she punched him in the face with all her strength, making him stumble back.

"Is that all you got, bitch?" Felix said.

"*No.* This is," Hill replied. Spinning around and pulling her Desert Eagle from her holster, she blew his brains out, sending him to the floor for good.

"Holy shit. Nice," Miller said.

Looking around the room, she saw Jacobs lying on the floor with a knife in his leg and Miller on the floor getting up.

"Where is Rachael?" Miller asked.

"She was right there. Brent must have gone after her," Hill said, her voice cracking.

"Brent went after Rachael? We need to save her," Miller said.

"Go after the president and Captain Craven. I'll take care of Brent. I promise," Hill said, heading out one of the exits after Brent.

Miller helped Jacobs sit up. "Are you all right?"

"Yeah, I'll be fine. Where'd Hill go?" Jacobs said.

"Hill went after Brent. I am going after the president for the data card," Miller said.

"Wait. You let Hill go by herself?" Jacobs said angrily, trying to get to his feet.

"No. Brent needs to be stopped, and we can't do this without Rachael. I'm going to first get Rachael and then the president. Agreed?" Captain Miller said, looking at Jacobs and checking his leg one more time.

"Agreed," Jacobs said.

Captain Miller went out the door to follow Hill.

Chapter 17

Rachael Morgan and Jessica Price

As Hill went through the last door into the parking garage, she saw Brent holding a knife to Rachael's face and yelling at her. Hill raised her gun and yelled at Brent, "Let her go, now!"

Brent pulled Rachael to her feet and positioned her between himself and Hill, holding a knife to her throat.

"Put your gun down, or I will kill this bitch," Brent yelled.

"Kill her, and I will put a bullet through your eye," Hill yelled back.

"Why do you want to save her? She started this whole thing, and I have proof," Brent said.

"If she did, put down the knife so we can talk about it," Hill replied.

"Put down your gun, and I'll put down my knife, and we will finish what we started in the office, bitch," Brent yelled.

Brent threw his knife to the side, still holding Rachael in front of him, and Hill threw down her gun. He threw Rachael against the pillar next to him, knocking her unconscious. Then he charged Hill, slamming into her. Hill used his momentum to throw him off and jumped up, landing a kick right to his chest that knocked him back. But he got to his feet and came at Hill once more, this time with a flurry of punches. Hill blocked them all and then countered with a punch to Brent's face, followed by an uppercut, knocking him back again.

Brent put his hand to his face, bringing back black blood. "I like a bitch who can hold her own," he said, wiping black ooze from his face.

This time, Brent blocked a few punches from Hill, catching her fist and striking two blows to her ribs. Brent felt her ribs break, and then he landed a punch to Hill's face, knocking her to the floor. Hill jumped up quickly, holding her left side where her ribs were broken.

"I also like a bitch who can take a punch," Brent said, smirking.

Brent attacked again, landing a few more punches to her stomach and another shot to her ribs that sent her to one knee. As Hill was on one knee, Brent kicked her in the chest, knocking her down flat on her back. Before Hill could recover, Brent jumped on top of her and started strangling her.

"Remember, this was where we were when someone hit me," Brent said with a chuckle, both hands around her throat.

Brent heard someone yell, "Hey."

He looked up to see Rachael wielding a knife. She stabbed at Brent's throat. He just managed to move to the left, and the knife sunk into his left shoulder instead. He roared in pain and let go of Hill to backhand Rachael, knocking her backward. Standing, he grabbed Rachael by the throat as she tried to stand and then slammed her against the wall. Throwing her to the ground, he kicked her in the stomach.

"I should have just fucking killed you, bitch," he yelled, pulling the knife from his shoulder. Black ooze dripped from the knife. "You can't kill me. I'm immortal, thanks to you."

Just as Brent took a step toward Rachael, three shots rang out behind him, and Brent fell forward, hitting the ground.

Captain Miller stood there, gun smoking. "Are you OK?" Captain Miller asked Hill and Rachael.

"I'm fine," Hill said, getting up and grabbing her side.

"Yes, I'm fine," Rachael replied, standing up.

"What the fuck is wrong with his blood? It's black," Hill said, looking down at Brent's body.

"He's infected," Rachael said. "How do we stop him?"

"Like this," Miller said, walking up to Brent's prone body. He pressed his gun against the back of his head and fired five shots. Black ooze flew everywhere, and his brains splattered everywhere. "Let's see him heal from that," Miller said.

Rachael put Hill's arm over her shoulder to help her walk and took her gun so Hill could hold her left side. They headed into the office to see how Jacobs was doing.

"Are you both all right?" Jacobs asked.

"I'm fine. It's Hill who needs help," Rachael said. Looking back, she saw that Captain Miller was gone.

"Where did Miller go?" Hill asked, noticing his absence at the same time.

"He must have gone after the president. What happened to Brent? Is he dead?" Jacobs asked, looking at Hill's ribs.

"Yeah, I wasted the fucker. He's dead," Hill replied, between short, gasping breaths.

"Looks like he gave you all you could handle," Jacobs said with a chuckle.

He taped up her ribs and then asked, "How's that?"

"It feels a little better," Hill said, looking a little better.

"Maybe I should just take a look at you, Doc," Jacobs said, turning around. But Rachael was gone.

"She went after them; she has my gun," Hill said, concerned.

Captain Miller hid behind some boxes watching Craven and the president talking to Jessica. The trio was standing just outside the door to the rooftop helicopter pad. As he peeked around the corner, he knocked down one of the boxes. The president, Craven, and Jessica looked around but saw nothing. Miller saw Craven disappear around the corner and assumed he had gone to check the roof.

He raised his gun and stepped out from behind the boxes. "Show me your hands, sir," Captain Miller yelled.

"Aw, Captain. How are you doing?" the president said with a smile.

"You need to stop them from killing anymore people before it's too late. I will be taking you into custody." He waved the gun between Jessica and the president to indicate that he meant both of them.

"On what charges, may I ask?" the president asked, lighting a cigar.

"How about genocide, for starters?" Captain Miller said.

"Genocide? I'm not the bad guy here," the president said, putting a hand in his pocket.

"Put your hands where I can see them. I don't want to shoot you," Captain Miller said.

Then he felt a gun press against the back of his head.

"Captain, please lower your gun. I don't want the captain behind you to kill you," the president said.

Captain Miller lowered his gun and cursed himself for paying too much attention to the president and not seeing Craven sneaking up behind him.

"As I was saying, I'm not the bad guy here. Your so-called friend Rachael Morgan is the one you should be going after," the president said.

"So, killing all those people at the camps was just mercy?" Captain Miller snapped angrily.

"No, it was for the survival of the United States. You heard Rachael. That so-called cure she came up with only suppresses the virus. Once one of them dies, they turn. Captain Craven has seen it personally. They had a man come into the medical tent who was having a heart attack. After dying, he turned, killing may people," the president explained.

"So, you decided to kill everyone?" Captain Miller yelled.

"Hey, asshole. That one guy who turned started an outbreak that killed over twenty-seven people," Captain Craven yelled back.

"Captain Miller, if we let them live, they are all a ticking time bomb that could kill hundreds if not more. Believe me when I say my decision to do this wasn't easy. There were kids as young as my grandkids in there. It was for the greater good." As the president spoke, he looked at Jessica.

Craven walked in front of Miller, still keeping the gun on him.

"Rachael started this whole thing. She helped the general release this infection. She needs to be stopped," Jessica said from behind the president.

"I don't think so," Rachael said, coming up behind Miller. "I told you and General Rhodes that the compound wasn't ready. And all the deaths Brent caused are on you, Jessica. You ordered me to inject Brent and his brother with Compound X because you needed healthy subjects."

"She consulted me before injecting him," the president said.

Hearing this news, Rachael looked surprised.

"Jessica, Brent went psychotic because of the injection. He was never like that. Not to mention those men you infected with Compound X, who would still be infected. If someone were to be contaminated with their blood, either by way of a wound or orally, this could start over, in a different country perhaps," Rachael said, pleading with her.

"I'm sorry you can't see the bigger picture," the president said.

Jessica handed him a gun, which he aimed at Captain Miller and Rachael.

Captain Craven turned toward the president and gave him a concerned look, "Sir, what are we doing here?"

The president fired, hitting Craven straight in the head.

Captain Miller yelled, "What the fuck are you doing?"

The president, still holding the gun on Rachael and Captain Miller, replied angrily, "He was growing a conscience. He just became expendable."

Captain Miller grabbed Rachael by the arm and ducked behind the box next to them, pulling her with him. The president fired again, but the shots went wide.

"I have the cure data card. Without it, can you remember the process for making the cure?" Jessica screamed.

The president fired on Rachael and the captain again, this time hitting the boxes next to them.

Just then, a Secret Service agent entered, guns drawn. The president yelled, "Apprehend Captain Miller and Dr. Morgan."

Jessica and the president made their way to the parking garage. They found Brent's body lying dead on the ground. They ordered the body to be brought to the lab at Ford Operating Base and placed in a top-secret lab so she could examine his body.

Back on the other side of the base, Secret Service agents found Captain Miller and Rachael. One of the men slammed Miller and then Rachael to the ground. Handcuffing both of them, the agents led them to a waiting chopper, planning to escort them to a nearby military base. As they walked, Captain Miller picked the locks on his cuffs. They loaded Rachael into the chopper. And just as they started to put him in alongside her, he hit one of them in the throat and punched the other, knocking him unconscious. Taking the other agent's gun, he pointed it at the pilot.

"Take off, or I will blow your brains out," he screamed, jumping on board.

The chopper took off, with Rachael looking out. Captain Miller picked the lock on her cuffs.

She looked up at him. "Now what are going to do? We need that data card. And in order for Jessica to make any more Compound V, she needs a live infected. There's only one place I know of," Rachael said, looking at Miller.

"Eagle's Nest. Marissa and the colonel," Miller said, a hand on her shoulder.

"My thoughts exactly," Rachael said, still looking out the chopper.

"They won't do it right away. They will have to clean up some of this mess first. But we need to stay low and hide. We need to go to the only place no one will go right now," Captain Miller said, thinking aloud.

"Texas," Rachael said. "I know another black site that is not used anymore. It has almost the same setup as mine; it's just a little out of date."

"Looks like we have a plan," Miller said, turning back to the pilot and telling him where to land.

Chapter 18

Cleanup

"Dear Americans, it pains me to have to talk to and about what is now known as the Outbreak in Texas. I am glad to inform you that the fugitives who released this infection have been dealt with. I know many of you have lost loved ones. My heart goes out to all of you." The president cleared his throat. "Cleanup has started. And for now, the state of Texas will remain under a strict quarantine. Anyone caught near or in a quarantine zone will be met with hostile action. This is for the safety of the public. I'm also glad to tell you that we have a cure for this infection, and every citizen will receive the vaccination so this tragedy won't happen again. We will be sending teams looking for survivors over the next few months. We'll also be making sure the infection has been eradicated. I promise you, we will rebuild and become a stronger nation. Thank you and God bless you all."

The president's address went out to the nation, and Captain Miller and Rachael watched on a screen in the black site.

"Why did he say we were dead?" Rachael asked, looking at Captain Miller.

"Because with us dead, it keeps the public panic down, and he becomes the hero. Also, he can keep send men in to search for us without raising the question of why they're sending so many teams into the quarantine zone."

"We need to get to Eagle's Nest before Jessica. If she gets to Marissa or the colonel, who are infected, she will have access to the compound. We also need to get that data card. I'm sure she will bring it to access Compound V," Rachael said.

"OK. You stay here. I will confront her. I just hope nothing has happened to Hill or Jacob. After Jessica, we will have to take down the president somehow." Captain Miller was angry as he recalled what the president had done. He gave Rachael a hug.

"Be safe," Rachael said.

As Captain Miller left the black site, Rachael feared she wouldn't see him again, and tears formed in her eyes.

"I need to go to the Eagle's Nest Facility to get the rest of the formula with the data card. Also, I'm remembering something Rachael said—something about Marissa turning after being inoculated. She may be infected and stuck in the facility. If so, she can be used to restart the research," Jessica said.

"Fine. But we need to deal with Hill and Jacobs. They know too much. They could become more trouble than they're worth to keep locked up," the president said.

"I'll take them with me. If they die in the quarantine zone, we could say they got infected," Jessica replied.

"Fine. Hurry. We need to finish making this cure to ensure that everyone is more at ease. My ratings are high with the people right now, and I would like to keep this momentum going," the president said.

Jessica made her way to an awaiting chopper. Leading Hill and Jacobs in cuffs and following in Jessica's trail was one of the biggest men they had ever seen.

"Are you going to kill us now?" Hill said angrily, trying to get at Jessica. But she was yanked back by the man holding her.

"No. You're going with us to Eagle's Nest. Then we're going to set you free," Jessica said, telling everyone to get on the chopper.

Captain Miller saw an incoming chopper and hid, trying to see who was coming to the facility. Hopefully, it was Jessica. As the chopper landed, he watched everyone exit the chopper. He saw Hill and Jacobs in cuffs being brought into the facility by what looked like a giant. He snuck under the chopper and planted a bomb, which he linked to a remote controller, before heading down the ramp to the facility. Once there, he waited by the exit, gun drawn.

Jessica and her men had finally managed to grab the infected, the one she remembered as Marissa, along with another one. She had her men secure them onto some rolling containers, strapping them down tightly.

"Good work, everyone. Load the infected on the chopper," Jessica ordered.

The men complied, but once they were near the exit, shots were fired over their heads.

"Everybody freeze," Miller yelled.

Everyone stopped and looked at Miller, some of them aiming their guns at him.

"This is between Jessica and me. Everyone else keep moving toward the chopper," Miller yelled.

"Go ahead. I will keep Mongo with me," Jessica said.

"Now, release Hill and Jacobs," Captain Miller said, looking at the thing she called Mongo.

He was wearing a mask that had skulls on it to make him look scary, and his huge arms looked like they could break a watermelon easily. He was standing behind Jacobs.

Jessica gave Mongo a nod.

To Miller, what happened next was so fast it was over before he could process it. Mongo reached out and broke Jacob's neck. Before he could grab Hill, she kicked Mongo. At the same time, Miller shot at Mongo, striking him several times in the chest. Black ooze seeped from the wounds. Hill hid behind some desks. Watching the black ooze run down Mongo's chest, the captain looked at Jessica, stunned.

"That's right. Say hello to Brent," Jessica said, grinning. "Where is Rachael?"

"She's safe. Don't worry about that."

"I guess it doesn't matter. It's only a matter of time. We will look in every black site and base, and we will find her. And when we do, Mongo here will kill her, just like he's going to kill you," Jessica said, nodding to Mongo again and walking toward the chopper.

"Before you go, I came across something in the general's orders that I think you should hear," Miller said.

Putting her hand up to stop Mongo, she said, annoyed, "Just come out with it."

"There was a flight that was never accounted for, flight 1720. It's on the sheets I looked up. It was headed to Paris," Miller said.

"Why am I supposed to care about this?" Jessica replied.

"There could be an entire plane full of infected. If they get released, we could be looking at another outbreak—one even bigger than Dallas," Miller said.

"If that happens, they will have to pay for the cure. Remember, it's a win," Jessica said.

"I guess you have a choice. Give me the cure, or I will blow up your chopper with your men and the infected you need," Miller said, showing her the remote he'd programed earlier.

"Stop. Fine. Here," Jessica yelled and tossed him a data card with the cure on it.

Miller caught the data card can and then tossed her the remote.

"I don't know how's that going to do you any good," Jessica said.

"Why? Is it fake?" Miller said, looking at it.

"No. But Mongo here is going to kill you," Jessica said, nodding again and continuing toward the chopper.

Mongo started walking toward Captain Miller. Captain Miller aimed his rifle and put a whole clip into Brent. It barely even fazed him. He went to reload, and before he could, Mongo grabbed the gun from him with one hand. And with the other, he picked him straight off the floor and threw him across the room.

"What the hell did she do to you, Brent?" Captain Miller said, picking himself off the floor.

Captain Miller ran straight at him and did a flying superman punch, landing it right in his face. It didn't even budge him. Mongo threw an uppercut, knocking Miller backward. Then he grabbed him by his throat and choke-slammed him into the ground.

Miller saw his bag on the floor and started to crawl toward it. Just as he grabbed it, Mongo/Brent grabbed his feet, pulling him up with one hand and punching his gut twice. With the third punch, he sent Miller flying into the wall.

Miller got to his feet and ran straight at Mongo again. He ducked Mongo's punch and pulled the pin on the grenade he'd managed to get hold of. Miller stuffed it into Mongo's shirt, jumping back as the grenade exploded, sending him backward and blowing the man formerly known as Brent into pieces.

Captain Miller got up. He grabbed his bag and the cure data card. Then he ran outside, holding up a remote controller just as Jessica's chopper lifted off the ground.

"Fuck you, bitch," he yelled.

Jessica looked down at him and then at her controller. "That piece of—"

Before she could finish her words, the chopper blew to pieces.

Captain Miller took out his phone. "I got the data card. We can get started on a real cure," he said.

"Great. See you at the facility in a few days," Rachael said, hanging up the phone. Rachael pulled out of her pocket the bright red vial Monica got from Nancy's blood and looked at it, thinking this was the real cure and she will show everyone what she can really do.

Captain Miller walked over to Hill and helped her out of her cuffs.

"Are you all right?" Hill asked.

"I'm fine. I need you to do something for me. I want you to bring this data card to Rachael. I need to take care of the president. He has to be stopped," Captain Miller said, handing her the data card.

Hill shoved it away. "No. I will take care of him. I owe him for killing my squadron. Also, you won't get close. I have friends on the inside who trust me and hate what he did at the border. They will let me inside. I'll do it. Rachael needs you; she trusts you. Besides, I'm expendable. Whoever goes is going to die."

Hill and Miller said goodbye and went their separate ways.

A week later, some of the president's Secret Service men led him through the door that came out of nowhere, telling him Jessica had come back and was waiting for him because she had news. The agent opened the door; the president entered, and he stood guard. Seeing a woman sitting in the dark, the president sat across from her. "Jessica, this had better be good, waking me up at this hour. And where have you been?" he said.

The woman turned around in the chair.

Hill pointed a gun right at the president's face. "You are a piece of shit. Go ahead and scream. No one will hear you here," she said.

"I assume Jessica is dead?"

"You would presume right. Miller took care of her. Now I'll take care of you," Hill said.

"Wait. I can bring you in, make you more powerful than you've ever dreamed, give you your own team. I can make you the leader of Raven Squadron. How does that sound?" The president smiled.

Hill lowered the gun. "That's the command I've always wanted," she said.

"Then its final. It's yours. And you will be promoted of course," the president said, now relaxed.

"Yes, but there's only one thing," Hill said, looking at him.

"And what's that? Anything you want," the president said, looking confused.

"Say you're sorry for killing my men," Hill said.

"Is that all you want?" the president said.

"On second thought," Hill said, lifting the gun and shooting him in the head. She spat on his body. "No apology would be enough for what you did."

Hill knocked on the door to the secret room, and the Secret Service man, James, opened it. Looking inside and seeing the president dead, he smiled at Hill. "Thank you. I lost my whole family at the border in Texas. He deserves this, not just for me but for everyone. Go. I will take the heat," James said, shaking her hand.

Once she was out of sight, he sounded the alarm.

Jason Mailey Lives in Council Bluffs, IA. Jason works for his family business and likes to write for fun on the side. He loves reading and listening to books.

This is his debut book.